"Amanda Marbais writes without fear about what passes in our society as the new normal. Every sentence reminds us how warm the water is while also insisting that we linger for just one more moment and then for just one more after that. These are marvelous stories."

—ANDREW ERVIN, author of *Burning Down George Orwell's House*

"In an American l: grime, scraped-ou  claw at meager p seems tentative an

relationships teetering on a razor's edge. Her leading women stare into the void of a post-recession world where men have become volatile waistoids. Danger lurks everywhere throughout this collection, and each story threatens to drive off a cliff. Marbais is a master of tension and gritty realism, but her approach is so unique, laced with absurdity and humor and flashes of surreal. The horror is so intense and inevitable that Marbais's characters tumble into its shadow. This collection is delightfully haunting and has tattooed a flickering neon junkyard into my brain."

—DUSTIN M. HOFFMAN, author of *One-Hundred-Knuckled Fist: Stories*

CLAIMING A BODY:

STORIES

AMANDA MARBAIS

Moon City Press

MOON CITY PRESS
Department of English
Missouri State University
901 South National Avenue
Springfield, Missouri 65897

The narratives contained herein are works of fiction. All incidents, situations, institutions, governments, and people are fictional, and any similarity to characters or persons living or dead is strictly coincidental.

First Edition
Copyright © 2019 by Amanda Marbais
All rights reserved.
Published by Moon City Press, Springfield, Missouri, USA, in 2019.

Library of Congress Cataloging-in-Publication Data

Marbais, Amanda
Claiming a Body: Stories/Amanda Marbais, 1972–

Further Library of Congress information is available upon request.

ISBN-10: 0-913785-66-9
ISBN-13: 978-0-913785-66-9

Cover illustration and interior design
by Charli Barnes, Charcoal Studio
Author photo by Ian McCarty
Edited by Karen Craigo

Manufactured in the United States of America.

www.mooncitypress.com

ACKNOWLEDGMENTS

Thanks to Mike Czyzniejewski, Joel Coltharp, Karen Craigo, and everyone at Moon City Press for their dedication to editing and publishing this collection.

Thanks to all the editors at the magazines where these stories first appeared: "Horribilis" in *The Collagist*, "Bottle Rockets" and "Tell Me" in *Moon City Review*, "The Calumet" in *Thuglit*, "Faker" in *Queen Mob's Teahouse*, "Werewolf DNA" in *Apalachee Review*, "Letter to Amandas" in *Hobart*, "Claiming a Body" in *failbetter*, and "Go Home" in *Pithead Chapel*. A special thanks to Kim Magowan for her expertise and encouragement.

Thanks to the writing group in Kansas who read my very first stories.

Thanks to all my creative friends who listened to my woes and my triumphs along the way.

Thanks to Janet Desaulniers, Rosellen Brown, Carol Anshaw, and especially Sara Levine for their guidance in my early days at the School of the Art Institute of Chicago. Their wisdom got me closer to the stories I wanted to write.

Thanks to Sara Wainscott and Sarah Meltzer for continually providing a place to read my work. Reading my work aloud was another way to own it and to reckon with its effects.

Thanks to friends and writers who have read these particular stories over the years, particularly Emily Anderson, whose input helped shape a few drafts and whose honesty made me a better editor.

Thanks to Antonia Gustaitis, whose exuberance as a reader is something I wish I could bottle and share.

Thanks to the folks at Tin House Workshop, particularly Elissa Schappell, for insights on "Tell Me." Thanks to Carmen Maria Machado for the encouragement and constructive feedback on this collection as a whole.

Thanks to Charli Barnes for the beautiful cover and to Jac Jemc, Dustin M. Hoffman, Leslie Pietrzyk, and Andrew Ervin for their generous praise.

Thanks to the supportive community at Loyola University Chicago—SCPS for their excitement in spreading the word about this new book.

Thanks to my son, Everett, whose sweetness and laughter is a real motivation.

My deepest thanks to Ian. His continual support has made this collection possible. He always inspires me to work past the doubts, frustrations, and fatigue. His humor brings levity, and his insights always open a new thread of undiscovered territory in a piece.

For Ian and Everett

CONTENTS

CLAIMING A BODY:

STORIES

CLAIMING A BODY

The woman's boyfriend agreed to go camping despite being called Needledick by her son.

Driving across the Iowa plains, the woman broke their silence with stories of her high school ski trips. She recounted bumming a waiter's weed and breaking her thumb in a collision with a ski instructor. She feathered a hand over her boyfriend's neck and laughed.

Her son turned toward the window and slipped in his earbuds, making it clear he wouldn't be asked to ski or rock climb or alpine slide or any other outdoor activity she had in mind.

The next day at the campsite, they sat in collapsible chairs and ate eggs from foil pouches among the milkweed and lupine. They watched the sunrise without a word. Finally, her son said he'd like to see the river.

"Stay close," she said. There were no other campers around, but last night the far off bawl of an animal had a quality like human weeping. And maybe the snap of branches and the pawing of earth meant a bear had been foraging nearby. She handed him bear spray and said to stay within 300 yards.

The trailhead was beautiful, hemmed with the blinding bones of white aspen before disappearing toward the river.

"He'll get a kick out of it." The boyfriend said this without conviction. "It might be fun to squeeze in a quickie." He already had a hand under her shirt. Prior to the boyfriend, the woman had been celibate for a year. Since they'd discovered each other's kinks, her desire had become unbearable.

An hour later, her son stumbled into camp, his cheeks smeared with dirt, his lips fluttering soundlessly. He'd uncapped the bear spray but hadn't deployed it, or at least there were no capsaicin burns. She thought, *Thank god*. But when she zipped his hoodie and their eyes met, she wanted to tear away her own skin.

He said, "There's a sick guy in the woods." His description centered on a foot, sweat pants, and "a horrible face." The woman freaked. Was the face chewed by animals? Were the eyes torn open, the sockets reduced to meat? Had her son seen down through muscle to bone?

The boyfriend would go look.

When he returned, he mumbled, "Maybe the guy passed out." But his wide eyes had an unnatural whiteness that nauseated her.

"We're calling the police," she said.

The boyfriend dialed immediately, but with the phone to his ear, he sounded nervous, like he needed the officer's reassurance. His neediness rankled the woman, since her son was now shivering and crying.

When the police arrived, she held the boy's reeking body close and inhaled the sharpness of weeds and sweat. His bones seemed to melt, and his rubbery arms slackened their hold around her waist. As the questions wore on, he wound down to monosyllables. She wanted to cram a hiking pole into the cop's mouth, because with each answer her son retreated, his eyes unfocusing until he'd all but disappeared.

The boyfriend brooded as they drove, and she sat in back, holding her son's hand as he stared out the window. They passed the bright plus signs of dispensaries, and she wondered if a pot brownie would be OK for a ten-year-old. What a thought! She was such an asshole. Her feelings of inadequacy returned, the same self-loathing she'd experienced with her miscarriages, and she braced for the inevitable waves of emotional reflection, like an autopsy she knew would last months.

At home, the boyfriend sat them on the couch. Here came all the clever ideas! He said he'd watched tons of forensic documentaries. He crouched forward, raised his hand, and sliced the air like a coach. He said hundreds of bodies go unclaimed for years. "People hike right by them in the woods. Lakes and ponds are filled with corpses, limbs inches from our legs as we're swimming around on Fourth of July or Memorial Day or whatnot."

"God. We swim right over them," said the boy.

The boyfriend was so sincere. But the woman gave him a look like—*Where is this going*? He went on, "This guy's family will get to see him again. They'll have a service. They'll bury him. You're a hero."

The woman willed him to stop talking. She wanted to grab a pillow and scream into it until the reverberations shot the feathers and dust and detritus out the other side. She wanted to shatter the windows with her rage.

☾

The woman and her son were in a Walgreens shopping for allergy medicine and trying be normal. But her son was staring, eyes unfocused, at what? Maybe razors. Maybe adult diapers.

"What's up?" she whispered.

"Do you believe that hero shit?"

Ignoring the word "shit," she said, "sure."

He half-smiled and said to the nearest guy in a red smock, "I'm a hero."

"OK," said the employee.

But for weeks he cursed at her, curled up on her bedroom floor whenever she slept alone. And in the morning, he recounted detailed nightmares of dismemberment, drowning, a plane crashing into the side of their house, a man beating her to death in an alley. The scenarios felt like TV plots, but her son's voice broke with each unburdening, and it bothered her that drama had become his reality. She missed the unremarkable days they'd passed together, before someone bludgeoned a man near his tent.

One night, he was sitting up in his sleeping bag in the center of the floor. He asked how long it took a person to "fall apart." The neighbor kid had a Cop Dad, and *he* said the weeds surrounding a corpse eventually absorbed trace amounts of blood, then secreted them out again in the cells of the leaves. "That's why they use the dogs," he said, "to find the scent even when animals pick the bones clean."

"That's unhelpful," she said.

"I knew you'd say that." He laid down again and pulled the zipper to his chin, cocooning himself in the nylon bag. "We're always alone," he said. "Other people have good advice, you know."

She got out of bed and sat on the cool floor beside him.

In the light from the hallway, her son blinked slowly. He told her that Cop Dad found the name of the victim, "Jay Fleming," in a database. "He was an only child," said the boy.

He repeated the name Jay four times like a ritual. "Do you think Jay's soul hovered over our tents that night?"

"Not sure I believe in a soul, Muffin," she said.

"Aren't you afraid of going to hell?"

"Not at all," she said.

"I am," said the boy.

"Jesus. That's dark," she said. "If you went to hell, I'd rescue you."

"Mom," he said. His voice was high, melting years from his life. Clearly, he pictured himself roasting in the flames of hell, skin blistering in the otherworldly heat.

She wished she could flog herself right there. She got back into bed and stared at the ceiling. Every night after this, the woman handed him a Benadryl and every night he took it with milk. The boyfriend thought this was wrong. The woman reminded him he didn't have children. Later, she would apologize for shouting.

He said, "Women have told me worse."

She slammed the cabinet door in answer.

A few nights of sleep made the boy less zombie-like. His energy returned, and he began riding his bike obsessively—to the park, to play laser tag, to the green belt by the river. Sometimes the neighbor kid with frothy red hair and the cop for a father rode beside him. But often he would take off alone on Saturday mornings and not return until dinner, his tires caked with mud.

☾

The boy sat at the kitchen table writing a school research paper he'd started with the Cop Dad. He told the woman and the boyfriend to "screw off" when they asked why. But then, as if unable to contain himself any longer, the boy excitedly told them the killer's motive had been a Toyota Camry and seven hundred dollars.

He used words like "sicko" and "scumbag" that the women felt sure came from the Cop Dad, and these black-and-white summaries of how people moved through the world seemed to make him both giddy and aggressive, and it pissed the woman off.

A teacher had helped him email Jay Fleming's family, and the family responded with their "deepest appreciation." They even mailed Jay's old belt buckle, which read "TEXAS to the BONE," and the son began wearing it every day and saying Jay was a part of him now.

"Disturbing," the boyfriend called it. He'd moved a file box of clothes into the woman's closet and now felt he had the right to an opinion. When she had opened the accordion doors, it stared at her like a deflated pair of forgotten underwear, and she said, "When did you get here?"

She found the boyfriend fixing the chain on the garage door. She looked up at him perched on the ladder. Each torque of the wrench revealed his soft white stomach and what looked like matted fur, which she found strangely appealing, and she thought of how he'd admitted to liking wax the night before, and that the trade-off of control felt like a kind of intimacy she hadn't known, maybe since college. For a moment she was grateful he was there.

The boyfriend noticed her smile, climbed down, and hugged her. He whispered that he wasn't a religious man, but that her son should talk to someone, a pastor or long-time friend. She noticed he stopped short of saying a shrink, and she appreciated that. She hugged him back, letting her body release in his arms.

An old Chevy pulled into the drive, and they both turned to watch her son jump out. He was crying.

The driver was forty-something, dressed in obscenely short cutoffs and a filthy sweatshirt. He gave her a look like *Lady, don't let your son ride home with a stranger.* Then, he popped the hatchback, pulled out a mangled bike, and handed it to the boyfriend. "I didn't do this." He directed his statement to the man and climbed back into his Chevy.

In the garage, they inspected the bike.

The son said it was a "piece of shit."

The boyfriend touched the broken safety mirror. She'd been meaning to get it fixed, and she gave the boyfriend a warning look about judging her. She held the boy.

The boy told them a truck had nearly hit him, and he'd thrown the bike off an overpass.

"Was anyone hurt?" said the boyfriend.

"Me!" said the boy. "I am hurt."

The woman's heart thundered in her chest, and she imagined walking slowly over the sloping shale bottom of a lake, her chin barely above water, a man clawing at the soles of her feet.

☾

At Christmas, the boyfriend floated the idea of a new bike for her son, but she bought him an iPhone instead. The boyfriend found the new phone hidden in a bag of old wrapping paper and a stack of forgotten holiday cards from ex-boyfriends. She had been meaning to throw the cards away.

He held out the bag and raised an eyebrow.

She said, "I have a past. Don't expect an explanation."

He shrugged and went to the fridge for a beer.

The woman wrapped the iPhone in bright red paper and gave it to her son early. She said if someone threatened him—point, shoot, record, all of the above. The boy looked satisfied and slipped it into his pocket like a talisman.

The boyfriend offered to drive him to school, and they frequently left at dusk, and she watched them from the front window.

When she first got the photos of a used condom, a broken tail light, and a thumb-shaped bruise at the base of a girl's neck, she thought her son's phone was stolen. Likely the images were taken during the commute or free period or just out a classroom window. But they seemed to be telegraphing a message she couldn't understand.

Her boyfriend said not to read too much into it. He was being "artsy." Although the condom thing "was odd," he had "seen far worse." Once one of the boyfriend's coworkers brought in pictures of his passed-out, naked girlfriend. "That's the shit a sociopath does," said the boyfriend.

How did he know the mind of a sociopath?

Half-submerged in her bath, stomach and thighs slick islands, the mother replayed the boyfriend's comment, and found new ways to detect violence in its subtext.

When her son was younger, everything was solved by plastic gates and outlet covers and nanny cams and oven locks and cordless shades. What if they eliminated everything that wasn't just the two of them? What if they could create an environment where everything was known and anonymous bodies didn't just float around in water waiting to be found?

In just her bathrobe, she grabbed a beer from the fridge, and walked outside to the porch swing and threw her body down, feeling as if she were tumbling into a ravine.

She sniffed a little, but she wouldn't cry.

"He's just commenting on the shit he finds deep," said the boyfriend. He sipped his beer.

She was aware of the boyfriend's heat, his weight on the swing, and she scooted to the opposite side and lay her head against the chain, allowing them to swing slowly to rest. "We could have had him stay in our tent," she said.

Before the camping trip, her son had argued so often for his own tent that she'd come to hate the words "tent" and "gross," which felt like a commentary on her as a person, an indictment of her roles beyond motherhood. But ultimately, she gave him his own space. They'd bought an old Coleman tent from the Salvation Army, and it had glowed a beautiful green from a battery-powered lantern, and it framed the strange silhouette of his body as he watched a movie on the iPad, while yards away a man beat a stranger to death with a Maglite and left his devastated body in the marl of riverbank and weeds.

"He'll work past it. He's seen bloodier things on TV," said the boyfriend.

"You think I shelter him?" She imagined how the boyfriend would parent based on months of comments. He used words like "honest" and "responsible." He'd find a horseback-riding camp or archery or football or field hockey. He'd have an answer. He'd definitely teach him to fix ham radios or gut deer or any of the other survival skills he embraced for the coming apocalypse, which he believed was near. She appreciated that he was skeptical about god and hell, and that he didn't see their intimate roles as fixed. But still, he was an outsider.

"Don't you shelter him?" he asked. "I feel like you've said this about yourself."

Without a word, she went inside to lie down. She spread out on her bed, her hands and feet stretched to the corners. She thought about the dead man's name in her son's mouth. She really hated the dead man.

For a month, the boy flooded her phone with pictures—a van packed with trash, a dead cat, another boy's purpled knuckles, two of them split. They came in intervals every three hours, just as the last ones faded from her mind. Now, at night, the boy asked if she'd seen them, and she exchanged a look that said she had. That was all they needed to say.

For a month, she weighed the contents of the file box in her closet. She tilted it, feeling the shift of the boyfriend's clothing, but never opened it. So she could never decide if it was actually lighter, and she said nothing about it.

One night after sex, the boyfriend un-cuffed her and kissed her wrists, and for a while they made out, but then she kept feeling like she would drift off. She curled away from him in the bed.

He traced the curve of her torso with his fingertip, performing on her what he liked best, to be touched in a way that was unsettling, yet tender. It was a touch that required her full acceptance, and she understood it had the type of discomfort that reminded one of being alive. He said, "It's going to be all right."

It wasn't. How could she expect him to understand? She was going to have to be better, stronger, more protective—ruthless, even. She didn't have the luxury of believing in ghosts or villains because all her son's life was a negotiation, and by extension so was hers.

She would tell him it was over, tomorrow.

She thought her boyfriend was asleep when he said. "I don't suppose you copied the keys?"

For a moment, she thought he meant the handcuffs, but realized he wanted keys to their house.

"Oh right. I'll do it tomorrow," she said.

He got up from the bed to have a cigarette and did not return. She found him on the couch the next morning. He was sprawled over the cushions, a man swimming through their living room, half-clothed, mouth open.

Her son stood beside him looking worried. He extended his finger and gently poked the boyfriend's bare shoulder. "He's OK, right?" he asked.

They watched the boyfriend's chest rising and falling as the woman sipped her coffee. "I think so," she said.

"Yeah. He doesn't look like Jay did," he said.

"Right," said the woman.

She tried to tell herself she didn't care if the boyfriend left, not at all. That everyone is remade over and over. And this is who they all were today. This was her son. This was her. Complicated, but alive. He could make of that what he wanted.

WEREWOLF DNA

One Christmas in college, I descended a fire escape in a snowstorm to avoid seeing an ex-boyfriend at a party. I had some of his stuff.

If I had lived in Switzerland during the first witch hunts, when some women were accused of being werewolves, I wouldn't have spoken up for them, even if I thought it was bullshit. I'm a feminist who avoids confrontation. In the fifteenth century, I'm sure I would have been the same type of person, and this somehow makes me worse than the persecutors.

That's why it's Friday night and I'm picking up my boss from the airport. He throws his roller bag in the trunk of his Denali and is visibly sweating by the time he hauls himself into the passenger's seat. He says, "Jesus, Nico. Thanks for picking me up. San Jose was a ball-buster."

I don't care about San Jose or his balls. Nico is not my name. It's Regina. Julian nicknames everyone for the first detail he notices. The week I started, I wore earbuds and mistakenly shared what was playing. My coworker is Pink Pants. There are thousands of reasons Julian is universally loathed in the office, not the least of which is this giant Denali I'm driving to pick him up.

"God, Nico, could you just like go through a Starbucks or something. I have a mega headache."

O'Hare's pickup lane overflows, and a security vehicle has lamprey-d to the bumper. There's no Starbucks before the city, but there's one in the airport, I'm sure. Of course, he couldn't stop. Julian leans back in the leather seat and exhales a cloud of cheap in-flight whiskey.

He doesn't remember. He has forgotten his meltdown, when he threw his iPad into a lamp in the conference room and yelled "motherfucker" at me. He glared at everyone like he wanted to scoop out their eyes. He kind of spit a little when he screamed, and the vein in his forehead threatened a possible stroke.

Now, he rips open a bag of airline pretzels and adjusts his pashmina. He's dressed like he's auditioning for a John Hughes movie: knotted sweater, leather boat shoes, feathery hair.

He starts reading his email, and for a minute, he just keeps saying, "Goddamnit. Oh, goddamnit." When his phone rings, he answers, "What's going on, Honey Butt?"

I hear his wife's muffled complaints. Julian pulls the phone from his ear, points to it, and smiles like he's getting away with something. He replaces the phone to his ear, says "Calm down, Katelynn," then extends it, just inches from my face.

We're stopped in traffic on 90, and I can make out that 12,000 is due for Jay's preschool bill, and she's "sick of being a single parent."

The last part is reasonable. But Julian just got off a binge at Sunsets, the strip club where he spent most evenings entertaining real estate clients. He used a company card, and I had to book expenses with the ultimate purpose of budgeting lap dances for the year.

"Listen. Listen. Can you hold on a minute? OK. I'm going to talk to the old man about a paycheck tomorrow. I'll call you back. Bye." He rests his head on the leather seat. "Don't have kids," he says.

"That's inappropriate." I say.

"Did I cross a line?" He says. "Do we need to call HR, huh, huh?" He lightly punches my arm. Being his operations director is like an episode of *Naked and Afraid*, a series of compromises, compounded with micro-humiliations.

"Seriously, Nico, take me to Lineman. It's easy to find. My buddy's texting."

"Shouldn't you go home?" I hate that I say this. It's none of my business.

"Yeah. I really need to unwind. Without kids." He looks back as if checking traffic. He often has an affectation of being distracted, when he actually is dying to share something. "We got big money rolling in," he says. "It's going to make you so happy, Nico."

"OK. But I gotta tell you about your dad. He gave me more checks for cabinetry and said to book them as commission. I have to report the sales tax." I feel like I've tossed a grenade at him. I wait.

"What?" He feigns surprise. He and his dad both force me to play mother to their preteen hijinks. Boys will be boys. I have the feeling they find it funny every time I raise a warning about sketchy business practices.

"I can't help you avoid sales tax," I say.

"Hey. I just got back. I don't know anything about what he did," says Julian.

AMANDA MARBAIS

He thumbs his phone and makes a call. "My brother,"
he says. This affectation is offensive, but it would take
a week to find the nerve to call it out. I want to puke
over my own silence.

"I'm about ten minutes away," he says "Later." He
disconnects, and I feel him staring. "Is something bothering you? Something personal? You seem all tense."

"I just don't want either of us wearing an orange
jumpsuit," I say.

"No. It's not that," he says. "The communication lines
aren't open, Nico. If we weren't in the car I'd give you
a hug. Is it hugging time?"

"Gross. Stop it," I say.

"I'm not being HR-friendly, am I Nico?"

"No, you're not."

"I'm just messing with you," he says. "Hey. Just drop
me off at Lineman. I'm going to take a nap while we
motor." He puts on his sunglasses, sits back, and says
nothing the rest of the trip.

That night, I loathe myself. All the way home, in a urine-
soaked train car, rocketing through the electric-blue
skies of Chicago, I can't shake the feeling I'm an idiot.
I've texted Luke, but spared him my internal struggle
over the latest humiliation. We're going through IVF, so
my moral guilt is nothing compared to our money stress.

From the L, Jefferson Park is an ocean of trees, glis-
tening in encased ice. Chicago's had a fickle spring.
You'd think Luke would be unwinding with hockey,
but he opens the door, holding a rocks glass with two
fingers of bourbon.

His laptop is open to donor profiles. The photo of a young woman with long red hair wearing a jean jacket stares back at me. I feel cheated on.

"Was he a nightmare?" he says.

"Yes." I yank my gaze away from the profiles. They make me want to shower.

"I'm already feeling around at work," he says.

"Yeah. That might be weird if you ask coworkers to find me a job," I say. I don't want to have this discussion. Employers who tend toward illegal acts pay larger salaries. "Close that," I say and point to the computer.

The profiles pics look like mugshots, women sitting and staring, with numbers beneath them. They are interlopers in our lives. Both of us are infertile, but like many aspects of reproduction, dudes come out ahead. The embryologist can isolate one tiny swimmer in a sea of the fractured and dying. One time Luke had blood in his semen and they were still like—"totally fine."

"I don't want you to have to go through it anymore," he says, following my gaze. He gently closes the computer.

"I don't want to talk about it." I lay down on the floor to pet the dog, my ultimate I-can't-deal move. The dog will take anything she can get. She starts licking my face.

"If I could do it, I would," he says.

This is such a stupid thing to say. No, he wouldn't. No one would. But I need to believe him. I need to believe he considers all the intangible costs.

"I just think we should stockpile money now. Pay for a baby one way or another." Even as it leaves my mouth, it sounds insensitive.

☾

Before Luke, I didn't consider kids. I'm still ambivalent. The other day my friend's kid ate an ice cream sandwich by lifting the plate to gnaw the cookie off the top. Gross.

Again, during the witch hunts, maybe there was a reason midwives were persecuted. Maybe some children crawled and squirmed and ate like werewolves. Maybe mothers and fathers didn't recognize their family at first.

At any rate, I am tired of hearing about my boss's kids. They are buoys on the tide of his insecurity. When he's down, they are nothing but a financial burden. When he wants a point of connection in the office, they are precocious geniuses with a tendency to mimic his quirks.

I think about this as we're having lunch.

Julian has finished a story about his son's need to say "Right on, yo."

"Wonder where he learned that?"

Julian leans against the window, sipping mezcal and eating foie gras tacos, which he ordered while I was in the bathroom. We're in an upscale diner, specializing in offal meat tacos, in a repurposed wooden booth, at a slick Formica table.

"Nico, I'm going to North Dakota," he says.

"The land of strip clubs," I say. He never sees himself as the butt of a joke, but always in on it.

"C'mon. I'm not going to any strip clubs." He wads up a napkin and throws it at me.

"Ow," I say without inflection.

"Yeah. Dad says I got to go there to oversee this first deal. Then, I got to see this other guy who just bought a franchise. Seriously. Good stuff. But listen, before I go, I wondered if you could cut me a check for like the next month with overtime. Thirty thousand. Dad says it's OK."

"You know, as owners, you'll both have to sign off," I say.

"Yeah. He's totally fine with it. Can you give it to Katelynn tomorrow? She'll have my balls if you don't."

They don't have the cash flow, but I don't know what to say.

Julian raises a finger. "We'll take the bill," he says. "That strip club thing is all about business, Nico. You wouldn't believe these guys. Sometimes that's all they think about."

"Your trip to Iowa last month, I looked up that two thousand dollar charge to the Lumberyard so I could job-cost it. Seriously. I don't want to see something like that again. I need warning."

"Oh, man. Sorry. But that's on you. The Lumberyard? That sounds like a strip club."

"Not for a company in the construction business."

"All right. Well, anyway. You don't mind waiting for the bill, right? Here's my card." He threw it at me. Julian always leaves when he gets uncomfortable.

I'm listening to Julian's dad Jerry talk to a Starbucks barista like she's twelve. When he finally gets back on the phone, he says, "How much does he want?"

"He wants …."

"Hold on. Hold on." Jerry makes small talk with someone he clearly doesn't know.

They're clones, both of them schmoozing all the

time. Both played Big Ten sports. Julian burned out on coke, and his father, Jerry, took his football team to the playoffs.

"How much?" he says.

"Thirty thousand."

In the office Pink Pants and Neal look up from their computers, necks swiveling toward me. Neal has already said he's thrilled Julian's on a trip. Julian calls him the Kremlin, which is so offensive, it's hard to wrap my head around Julian's nerve. "Thirty thousand?" Neal mouths. I nod.

"All right. I never agreed to that, you know," he says in his gravelly voice.

"What do you want me to do?"

"I guess cut it. When did he say he needed it by?"

"Tomorrow."

"Jesus. Do we have the cash?"

"Not this week."

Pink Pants shakes his head.

"Well, just don't pay our insurance. We'll mail that check next week."

I get off the phone and roll my eyes.

"Big boy gets his money, huh?" says Neal.

"It's not funny," I say. I take the check to the printer. "I don't want my paycheck to bounce."

"I, for one," says Pink Pants. "don't think a damn thing he does is funny."

"Word," said Neal

"Both of you shut up," I say. It's like Neal and Pink Pants are so young they don't get it. We all need to be paid, which typically means Jerry will make a last-minute deposit to the company.

At this point, I wonder if the genetic bond is impossible to fight. In my limited experience, I've seen two families cover crimes for their children—once when I was a teenager, and my friend committed a hit-and-run, and many times in Jerry's business.

The strengths of the genetic tie makes me nervous about carrying someone else's kid. Am I breaking some kind of cardinal rule? Is there some kind of karma-based punishment for this? I know I'm being stupid, but will a kid grow to hate me? Julian already seems to hate Jerry, so there's the potential for parental torture either way. Maybe, for a little while, Luke and I can pretend.

Luke holds the shot like a dart, the way he was taught by a tight-lipped nurse.

My legs are dotted with dime-size bruises. This is my 163rd shot of hormone or hormone antagonist. I've given 83 vials of blood and had 40 transvaginal ultrasounds. I've had my fallopian tubes filled with dye. I've had my uterus punctured with 12-inch needles, and once, I accidentally awoke during surgery. On the last round, my ovaries fattened, fell over, and lay on my bladder, giving the sensation of a knife in the back. I've gained ten pounds; I've lost ten pounds. Most weeks I'm sick.

But this history doesn't have to be spoken.

The act makes Luke say, "It's not fair."

I shrug my shoulders. "I'm trying not to think about it."

"I know," he says. He jabs the syringe of Lupron into my thigh, then gently rubs the skin.

"Did you feel that one?"

"No."

"Good."

He throws the syringe in the bright red mini-trash can and hands me a shot of Buffalo Trace he's already poured and set on the sink. We don't always do shots after shots, but this is the last Lupron. On Lupron, I forgot how to spell his last name. For that 5 seconds, I was terrified.

"If this doesn't work, we can get a sperm donor."

"If this doesn't work we're going for adoption, which is probably what we should have done in the first place." The shot burns.

He looks hurt.

"That's not an indictment of what we're doing now."

"I love you."

"I know. I love you," I say. It's not that I don't. It's that I was happier before, and hope I will be again. The problem isn't him, it's my inability to tolerate my life right now, in this moment, and my job is the least of it. I know I need to say this. He can take it.

At two a.m., after drinking with potential clients at a West Loop club called Sway, we're parked outside Julian's darkened two-flat. "Go in for me," he says. Drunk, head resting on the cracked taxi seat, Julian's cheeks appear bloated, his skin a rich pink that might make a nervous friend worry he is in cardiac distress. I'm guessing he just needs to throw up.

He wants his day planner and a cache of worn business cards. Tonight, Julian and Jerry worked each other up over some vendor who bought two hotel franchises in the Dakotas. They fed each other, saying what each wanted to hear, ending each other's sentences, until they'd determined they'd make a wild amount of money.

"You want to drunk dial?" I say.

"No."

"It seems like you do."

He sighs, a kid winding up to say something inappropriate, a verbal abuse designed to elicit guilt and fear. Julian's animosity for technology has created this quandary. If he had the contact in his phone, he wouldn't even need me. But Julian's Luddite behavior has become an intractable personality trait. At his worst moment, he mistakenly deleted every file in Dropbox and hid in the conference room when his dad found out.

"You don't want to just go inside, go to bed?" I say.

"No. I have to meet someone after we drop you." The cab driver is on his phone, oblivious. Julian throws his head back against the seat again. "C'mon."

Maybe because I just negotiated for overtime, I feel I can't say no. I snatch my purse, from the seat. What hell is wrong with me?

"Nico," he says through the open car door. "Don't wake up Katelynn and the kids. She'd fucking freak."

"No shit." Emboldened by my impertinence, I turn toward the house.

I unlock Julian's front door with the keys, punch in the code—CUBS. I should have known after he'd downed five shots of Basil Hayden, when he began lobbing laconic quips about money, when he leaned farther back in the leather booth, his chest inflating, that he'd become what Neal called the Man-Child. Ultimately, I would have to take care of him.

Their open floor plan loft soars two stories and is floor-to-ceiling pink granite and cherry wood. Seven hundred and fifty thousand dollars of oddly inviting space, with the veneer of a Marriott lobby. In the day, it was less shadowy, less cluttered with the gray shapes of plastic toys.

Katelynn would call the cops if I woke her. She wanted my job, believed she and Julian could work together. She wanted to replace everyone with her friends.

He'd said it was "in the front hall shitter." Off the kitchen, I feel around for the door handle, the image of a thief.

I have two minds on Katelynn and Julian's marriage. Katelynn knows about the strip clubs. She turns in expense reports filled with lap-dances from their personal cards. But one day I came in the office, and they are arguing about a condom on the passenger floor of the company car, which Julian blames on Pink Pants.

Their relationship may be on the rocks, but they're united in draining the company.

The bathroom is a landscape of neglect: several sizes of underwear dotting the floor, a half-eaten hoagie on the sink, the planner on the toilet tank. I'm holding the planner, when I imagine a noise, deep in the condo. I stand still, as if stillness will help me hear.

It's human shuffling. I text Julian—*Someone's up*. I clutch my phone waiting for the buzz.

I sit on the toilet for three minutes, planner in hand.

While I wait, I thumb the planner. Normal Julian-bullshit, but then on Monday—names, times, notes. In Julian's sloppy handwriting the actual word—interviews. He's scheduled at least four interviews, and I realize he's firing someone, maybe gutting the whole place. One of the interviews is a project manager at his buddy's company.

I text again—*Hey dude. Come save me from your wife.* No answer.

I listen, focused on deciphering sounds: wind against the condo, the footsteps of a child, or Katelynn. A child means I'm cool. I decide to wait ten minutes and set my phone timer. I read the planner. The next week has another set of interviews. If he's firing me, I'm going to kill him.

When Julian threw the iPad shattering a lamp, he finished screaming, "You are all insensitive worthless shit." I wouldn't make fake invoices to save him two hundred thousand in worker's comp violations. After confronting me, his anger passed, an electric current, to the first person through the door—Neal. He called Neal a cocksucker.

"Calm down, Jules. Calm down." Seated at the conference table, Jerry's voice grew shaky.

"Dad, everyone in this office hates me. And they won't do their fucking jobs."

"Son."

"Don't tell me it's not true." Julian looked like he wanted to shiv Jerry in the neck.

Jerry expression grew sallow. He covered his cheeks and his mouth with football-player-sized hands. "Let's not go to the place," he said, almost in a whisper. He looked at me, helplessly. His craggy face sank in disappointment, an expression he would wear for weeks.

Julian flushed purple. "Fuck you all," he said. "I'm going home."

Jerry didn't stop him. "Oh, Julian" was all he said. First thing Monday, Katelynn arrived and asked to sit with all of us, watch us work.

I'd intended to quit. I needed the money. I held the planner. Again, I imagined killing Julian. The noise started, there was definitely someone outside, a shuffling, light as a rabbit from the hall.

My phone buzzed. *Met buddy at Twisted Spoke. Come over if you want. She'll go back to bed.*

My thumb hovers, ready to text—*I know you're firing everyone.* I want to ask him why he only cares about himself. I want to text—*I quit.* But I put my phone in my pocket. It's been fifteen minutes. If I'm going to get caught, at least I won't be stuck in this filthy bathroom.

When I open the door, a crack, I see two eyes staring back, a mat of black curly hair. "Mommy?"

Jay holds a plastic robot under one arm, and his raised brows suggests he recognizes me, if not by name. I feel pretty satisfied he knows I'm not a thief or a murderer.

Still, he's troubled by my presence. He clutches the robot. "It's bad," he says.

I kneel on the floor and stare into his small pink face, large cheeks. I set the planner at his feet. "They're bad," I say. "They're actually real assholes."

It occurs to me I would make a bad mother, that a bad mother could be persuaded to sneak into someone's house, curse at a kid. I walk toward the train, thinking to myself, I'll make some kind of mother. I don't know what kind. If the kid is not a better person than me, I hope they're stronger.

HORRIBILIS

One evening, I ran over a cat. Upon impact, its flat eyes reproached me, like it hadn't known pain before. I got out of the car, stood in the headlights, and cried. It had a crushed skull and its bloody ID read "Sparkle-Motion, 5502 Ashland Ave." I delivered it to an angry mother and a six-year-old, wearing Dark Knight pajamas, who gave me the devil's look. I'm a vegetarian!—I wanted to say. He wouldn't buy my sincerity. It was horrible. His reproach appeared in every human expression. My insomnia returned, and I went to my shrink.

My shrink was into alternative medicine. She had posters of people standing on cliffs, their arms raised in a V. Tuning forks lay on squares of bright orange cloth. Lamps were buried in large amber rocks. She wore blouses with choir-cloak sleeves and full-rimmed hipster glasses.

She had once been on Broadway, but never gave details about her roles. She assured me she was never hired for a lead, and eventually she grew tired of being poor. Her colleague had been a massage therapist for Kiss. This explained their lively office punctuated by flighty laughter. My shrink was laid back, and this appealed to me.

AMANDA MARBAIS

"You hit a cat. How horrible. I would be so upset."
She was never one to deny validation. She adjusted
her glasses. "OK so how is your anxiety level?" She lit
some incense.

"Terrible."

Phobias are the most common mental illness, yet I
had an uncommon number. They can be broadly clas-
sified as anxiety disorders, and this was my diagnosis.

"So which fears are bothering you?" she said.

"All. All the fears," I said.

"Uh-huh," she said. She broke out the tuning fork.

In my household, my shrink gained celebrity status
the summer she helped my husband Eli through a
job change. She was often called upon to assist in
minor issues.

"So do you want to go?" I said.

"Yes," said Eli. "If you don't mind."

The need for a session arose from our enjoyment of
a certain kind of pornography. It was about jellyfish
and people getting stung during sex. These productions
involved *Magnum PI*-type settings, bad acting, and
then frantic jellyfish stinging. We had stumbled on to it,
and while appalled at first, we just continued watching
and were eventually turned on. We'd been watching it
for weeks, doing it when the jellyfish stopped.

Yet there was a drawback to discussing sex. My
shrink was like my mother.

I met Eli post-shrink, years after accepting a bad
childhood. By even the most lax standards, my parents were not the Keatons, unless there's an alternate

universe where Steven and Elyse engage in all types of abuse: physical and emotional. My parents were absent *any* type of moral compass, even say a Jim Jones one.

When we arrived at the office, Eli took in the new posters, the aromatherapy candles, and the wish box, but said nothing. He and my shrink immediately caught up with banter.

Hitting the cat sent me into agrizoophobia, with a special fear about bears. We lived in the city but vacationed in national parks. Agrizoophobia rode my established neurosis like a pilot fish. While fixated on an object of fear, I'd repeat "motherfucker" like Samuel L. Jackson whenever I saw a cat, bear or someone who looked like Lou Reed.

"Do you feel anxious all the time, or just uneasy in general?" She was opening a package of eagle feathers.

"It's a real phobia this time—swear to god."

Most people harbored a crumb of phobia regarding something—the roar of cars, fireworks, wormholes, sweating crowds at county fairs, spiderwebs, giant squid, etc. Once I had a phobia about manholes, a splinter of Cacohydrophobia.

My therapist specialized in anxiety treatments. Long ago, she'd studied with Francine Shapiro who had developed EMDR, a therapy utilizing REM. My shrink's office was an anti-anxiety-lair equipped with gear—giant headphones and moon-shaped glasses, like those worn by Geordi La Forge. Patients chanted pleasant tropes while watching a sea-green balloon float away.

She was hinky, but interesting. However, on my

walks through Ravenswood to the train, I wondered if people could ever really know each other. Because, if anything, she knew me better than my mom. Of course, there wasn't actual equality or shared experience. So of course, we didn't really know each other, which seemed surprising after sitting in her chair for six years.

Ailurophobia soon became an issue, and purring became a total detonator for me. We couldn't visit our best friend, Michelle, because she had two cats. One was a Maine Coon the size of a bobcat, a motherfucker of twenty-eight pounds with a five-inch bat-tail. When it jumped, it shook the floor, and its meow resembled a drunk guy mocking a meow.

I developed a fear of true crimes shows, the ones deeply imbedded with the message "It really could happen to you." from the owl attack to the man waiting in the closet. I feared everything from an owl attack to a man waiting in the closet. I feared the kidnapping from the street, only to lose your cell phone before being thrown into an Oldsmobile trunk. I feared dismemberment.

On my way home, I saw a terrifying cat and swerved before going into hyperventilation. To have a cat phobia is to not be able to use the Internet. Eli looked up from his computer when I said this.

"It's all porn and cat videos," I said.

"Don't I know it," said Eli.

Someone posted a cat meme on Facebook, and I had become transfixed. "It's horrible," I said. "Horrible."

He looked over my shoulder. "That's because the cat is Photoshopped to look like Nicholas Cage. That's both amazing and terrifying." He closed my computer for me. "Who would do that?"

"I feel like I'm entering crazyland," I said.

Eli and I shared one phobia. We went camping and because of the mild winter were beset by ticks. One gave Eli Rocky Mountain spotted fever. "It sounds more like a craft beer than a disease," he said to the doctor.

He began taking antibiotics. The next morning as Eli held our dog, a motherfucker dropped to the floor with a wettish thud. It looked like a rock with legs, or what I imagined could be a polyp on a dying man. We found another twenty-six, and disposed of seven at a time with tweezers and a jam jar. We both grew phobic about ticks, but sharing made the fear surmountable.

But after six years of therapy, ultimately my fears grew worse. I made a catalogue: spoons, fireworks, dresses that don't fit, bank lines, viruses, manholes, ink spots, trains, apple-picking, golf courses, Mary Lou Retton, bowling, Super-Soakers, lampshades, firearms, glass tables, etc.

On my next visit, my shrink shocked me by not asking about Eli. She had left our last appointment behind— one more proof she had a life. She stood below her "Hydration is the key to life" sign and filled her water bottle from her new pink cooler. She wore a knee-length smock embroidered with ferns. She quaffed her water bottle. "What about doing some inner child work?"

"Oh. Jesus. No," I said. I stared at the hand puppets of Jung, Maslow, and Freud, the Tibetan singing bowl, and her reed diffuser. I wouldn't look at her.

Really she was suggesting soul-retrieval. Good thing Eli wouldn't be weirded out, because I would definitely tell him later. It would be more fun to laugh with him about it than to do it. Everything seemed a drag. "So we're contacting the four-foot-tall cunt-bag?" I said finally.

My shrink lit some incense. "Now cunt-bag, that's a name."

Under full meditation, I focused on the memory of the woods. Its young trees and dry leaves obscured the ranch houses. The inner child jumped down from a low branch and bit my neck, and though spoonlike in bluntness, her baby incisors broke skin. "Motherfucker," I said, but my eyes were closed.

"What's happening?"

"She bit me."

"She must be frightened."

"Or she's a bitch!" I looked at my shrink like she was crazy.

"Tell her it's OK, that she can't bite."

"Don't bite, bitch!" I said.

"I don't think talking to her that way is going to help. Maybe you should ask her what's wrong." She waved more incense at me and smudged it with a feather.

"Bitch, what's wrong!?" I shouted.

My shrink snickered. "Sorry," she said. "Tell her if she comes out of the woods, you'll give her something she wants, like a pony or something."

"Really, is that good therapy? I can't give her a pony."

Yet secretly, I wanted a pony.

"It's in your imagination. You can give her anything you want."

We coaxed her past the neighbor's house. There's nothing worse than having to tell a kid, "You're screwed. Whichever direction you go, you'll be exploited. That's your destiny, and you'll hate it."

"Now all we have to do is retrieve your soul," said my shrink. Her embroidered smock made her dyed hair unusually red.

"Should we whistle for it?"

"It does sound funny doesn't it?" She laughed.

"OK." I told Inner Me the truth in a laconic, controlled way. But it was the pony that lured her to ride like SheRa across an Indiana suburb, vaulting over the community pool.

"Do you feel better?"

"Somewhat."

My inner child was supposed to settle into my apartment with an imaginary room, and the pony, in an imaginary stable. I've done this a good fifteen times. Soul-retrieval is the New Age-y name for it—I err on the side of Carlos Castaneda in his somewhat grounded anthropological days.

"Well, don't be surprised if you feel a little more anxious this week." She gave me an awkward hug.

On the drive to meet Eli at Michelle's, I actively forgot everything.

"Just touch the cat," said Michelle. She had the Maine Coon on a table, as if she were grooming it. "Seriously.

Just touch it," she said. It turned and growled.

"It's fucking growling at me."

"It's just scared," said Eli.

"OK. I don't want to force you," said Michelle. "I feel bad."

"Yeah," I said. "Sorry."

On the way to the party, our failed immersion therapy left me hypervigilant. I didn't mention this week my fear was polio, which could explain my fever, stiff limbs, and back pain. It didn't seem irrational. I considered it in aggregate of an hour per day: in the bath, on the train, walking to work. Polio. I knew I would die, so was I above deadly diseases?

On Monday, I became obsessed with shooters. My office building contained a catacomb of government branches. Last year, a man brought his seven-year-old to the Social Security office. He waved a gun and demanded Arnold's Spare Ribs, a Barq's, and seven hundred dollars in back Medicaid costs. The elevators were cordoned off and bomb dogs sniffed the bathrooms. My fear was not totally irrational. The guy *was* owed seven hundred dollars, because Social Security was wrong. But for days I pictured my office door bursting open and someone blasting my face.

I did not tell Eli as I slid into bed. It was raining. He had gotten us diner food and lit a candle in our kitchen nook, which overlooked the Oak Park street and a backdrop of Victorian houses.

He researched backpacks for a trip to Montana. He had gotten a raise and found a deal on flights.

"We can camp up there, backcountry, then stay in this railroad chalet."

"There's more chance of bear attack in backcountry. You watched *Night of the Grizzlies* with me," I said.

"You have more chance of being struck by lightning. I'm not giving you a hard time though," he said.

My fear could be traced to obsessively watching *Grizzly Man*, a documentary about Timothy Treadwell, whose celebrity was derived from the infamy of his bear-related death.

"Well, we don't have to," said Eli. On the nightstand beside him were his pocket knife and the remnants of the strap he tried to repair.

On an alpine ledge, the chalet offered a view of archaically named natural phenomena—Gunsight Mountain, Lake Ellen Wilson, Bad Marriage Mountain, and Beaver Chief Falls. This place seemed appropriate for rail men, 1920s moguls on wooden skis hiding flasks of gin, and hikers. Eli clicked through the Flickr.

"I don't want to be resistant to things because of fear," I said.

"Maybe we need to go someplace where there are no natural predators," said Eli.

"I can do it," I said. But I couldn't do it. There was no way. Months of therapy would have to prepare me.

I have a phobia about the world ending. I imagine a visit to my favorite news outlet will yield a slide show in which the world's end is a horrifying photo available for five seconds. Thousands of birds will have fallen from the sky and bats will have lost their nocturnal radar and slammed into buildings. Magnetic fields will have disappeared, and an asteroid will be headed for North America. It will release thermal radiation. Everyone's fingernails will fall off. Weather patterns will change. The water will be contaminated. It's going to be in a streaming slideshow of death.

"How have you been feeling?" said my shrink.

"I've been thinking about the end of the world."

"That's dark."

"Well," I said.

"No one really wants to die alone. That's probably your fear," she said. "OK. More to the point, is she home safe?"

"Yeah," I said.

I left feeling light-headed and quickly walked to a bakery to buy a peanut butter Twinkie. Already I had forgotten my shrink, the event evaporating in the street. I resented having to deal with it. I resented her.

We planned our vacation to Sperry Chalet in backcountry. We flew to Kalispell and stayed one civilized night in a railcar, a restored caboose in which we took long showers, and then we lay out flat on the clean bed and watched the Amtrak pull up and the people get out with their packs and trekking poles in the extended dusk. Rested, strapped with backpacks, we hiked Gunsight Trail, tracing the cirque of remaining glaciers. The rivers became creeks below the mountainside. A John Ford movie landscape, boulders were the size of cars, cliffs exceeded skyscrapers, and meadows diminished us to ant proportions, as if we simply crossed a city park.

In a pine forest, we climbed through bear grass, monkey flowers, fireweed. We crossed a fast-rushing river where it grew narrow. In many spots, the river gushed, an open hydrant thickening to a waterfall cascading the hill. Eli talked loudly to scare off bears, then switched to whistling show tunes. I realized "Singing in the Rain" seemed utterly appropriate for scaring bears.

I knew the origin of this technique. Other than people with exotic pets, lone hikers were most susceptible to annimal attack. A ranger warned us of silence, claimed running while listening to earbuds could lead to death.

We camped on flat terrain near the rushing river. Even black bears have attacked campers at night, ripping their tents and dragging them by the rib cage. "It's rare," said Eli. He patted my arm. I didn't sleep well for the first hour, but with a Valium I was out.

Bears' chiefly vegetarian diets comforted me. They were only violent if desperate, freaked out, or if they were just an asshole bear. They mapped their habitats, knowing every stone and every tree. They could walk a hundred miles from home in search of food and were still tough enough to return to their den in just a handful of days.

"Where did you hear all that?" said Eli as he climbed a hill in front of me.

"Animal Planet."

"God. You're cute," he said.

"I am kind of embarrassed by my sources." Still I went on. "They're unpredictable, though. And they're smart. They know we're not to be trusted. Did you know they can run up to thirty miles an hour?"

"We're not going to see a bear." He cupped his hands, shouted, "No bears."

Cresting the hill, he turned and smiled, beautiful though damp with sweat.

Still, I imagined wide-set eyes, elongated snouts, longer claws, and humped backs. But their specificity was sacrosanct. They could be all gradations of brown and black and above all elusive.

When we did see the bear, it was rust colored. It vaulted the trail's width, like a tumbling ball, disappearing in the brush as if chased. It filled me with joy and exhilaration, as I stared at the undulating brush.

The second one moved slowly, an explorer pushing aside branches as if peering—angry at the hubbub of people. When he moved into the trail, his head lulled as if heavy with chuffing. He filled the trail. He bobbed a "no" and then charged. My limbs floated. Everything slowed. I collapsed in the bear grass. Eli already lay in repose like a child, his face damp. Most of my life had been a string of phobias, and now I could think of nothing but bear grass. As I heard the bear gallop toward the hillside and dive through the brush, I thanked nothing, but gazed at Eli in the silence.

BURIED

Each week, I leave work at the Crossroads Hotel when the lobby roars like a jet engine. My boss doesn't believe noise pollution is a thing, though he's seen the gas fires. I finish budgeting, take his calls at Shoney's—you know home of the Big Boy.

Not only does Shoney's still exist, but it has super-soft glazed donuts, a seriously stocked salad bar, coffee, and WiFi. It spares me from working in the Rambler I share with Carl, who is close to breaking up with me. I like to avoid breakups. They generally mean the other person provides a laundry list of my unpleasant and often suppressed qualities. Screw that.

Shoney's parking lot is a dangerous island of truck-sludge and snow mountains, courtesy of the crew who daily plows the strip mall but apparently raises the middle finger to the Big Boy. I'd been stuck twice. Carl and my brother, Steve, asked why I still go there. "It's nasty," says Carl.

"It doesn't smell like fracking chemicals," I tell him.

Even a small criticism of fracking, the most loaded topic in Williston, annoys Carl. I doubt our end will be amicable. Bad news for my brother, who's become so close to Carl, I question what goes on when I'm not around. I kind of wish it were sex, but I worry it is something illegal.

Inside, the hostess Kara leans on the counter eating a cream-filled donut the size of a coyote's tail as she talks on her cell. When there's only a handful of women in town, you feel like you got to be friendly. I try to catch her eye, do a two-finger wave, but she turns away. Kara is going through some stuff. She isn't ready to get divorced. Life's shitty, Kara. I keep this thought to myself.

Steve generally knocks off work at Bakkline and comes here. He likes to throw himself into my booth with a melodramatic sigh, smelling of ethanol and Bag Balm, that stuff they put on cows. Every day he tops my coffee with Fireball without asking.

Today I put my hand over my precious Shoney's coffee. "You look worse than usual."

"Quinn Brothers is closing."

Steve and the other drillers obsess over shale company closures, unspool them like the numbers on a Dow Jones display.

He lives with five drillers who are edgy about getting canned. We all went to Darcy's last week. They were a laugh riot. Normally, his roommates like to go to the Romeo Lounge or the Liberty Evangelical Church. At Darcy's, McGraw playing, they did shots and complained about everything including the winter. You know, the shit you can do nothing about.

Of course, the obsession now is the driller, the family man with a two-year-old in Ohio, who has gone missing.

"Carl's really concerned. But you both didn't know this guy, right?"

"It's a small community," says Steve. "Guy had a kid." At six-foot-eight, Steve hunches in the booth, like an adult on a playground seesaw. His face contorts with concern.

"Yeah. Well, Carl's pretty depressed. He hasn't even cleaned out his cereal bowl in a week. It's like super crusty." I proceed to tell him how Carl lies around streaming Homeland and drinking Red Stag from a Staples mug, coiled beneath a sleeping bag, putting the full weight of his body against the cold camper window. "That shit could break, and winter's only started."

"Don't make it an inquest," says Steve. "He's depressed because a decent dude is missing. You know about that." Steve's expression is wilting.

Last week, I told Steve about my insomnia, how the amber alert fliers remind me of his high school girl-friend who went missing at seventeen. She went for a hike in Estes Park. No foul play, but she was rappelling off a steep cliff, lost her hold.

Watching Carl grow depressed over the driller made me think of those months of worry in high school. Maybe the pain we have in common is bringing us together. Our family bonded over the search for Melissa. Maybe Carl and Steve are growing closer over the idea of some dude walking away from the man camp and maybe freezing to death, or maybe something else.

"I'm being insensitive. I see that now."

"Stop thinking too hard about this," says Steve. "If they find him, it won't be pretty."

The next night in my Pathfinder, Carl checks the rearview obsessively, but he doesn't talk to the bloody driller curled like a dog in the back seat. We are trying to decide if the police followed us from the bar. My breath chugs in tailpipe clouds, and I shove my hands between my thighs.

Out the windshield are the torches of gas, a hedge of methane explosions an indeterminate distance away. Rust-colored plumes like fat cotton rolls, deceptively soft. The ambient glow of the Lion's Den Adult Bookstore and the Walmart.

"I just want to go the hospital," says the driller. He uses Steve's wool hat to soak up the blood.

"Shut up," says Steve.

I start a little at this, grip the steering wheel. Steve is a weirdo, but not rude. Unfortunately, his face is shadowed, and he turns toward the window.

He was hyped up that night. When the bar erupted in shouts, he was part of the crowd of drillers pushing toward the fight, moving tables aside. One minute we were in a not-unpleasant loop of Tom Petty tracks and Fireball, and the next, the cops started shouting to "Get down."

I stood near the bar, and Randy, the bartender, shoved a stack of money at me. "Put this in your pants," he said.

Gross. I mean, not the worst. I was the only woman nearby and the cops weren't looking at me. This town has a chasm between genders, an undercurrent of assumptions and belligerence, like a middle school dance. I shoved the money in my pants, walked past the police officers, feeling light-headed, aware of the transgression, maybe feeling a thrill from it.

We drove around Williston. For a while, we parked behind a darkened Outback, texting Randy, like "Hey dude. What do you want done with this money?" Then we just drove to the trailer, the driller collapsed in the back seat, nothing but groans and whimpers.

Not like this driller hadn't been into it. He pushed the other driller against the paneled wall, and as he threw punches he shook his head like he was saying "no," like there was power in his own inner conflict. He'd raised his hands to his face, knuckles purpled and chewed.

"He'll probably be fine at home."

Steve is silent, though Carl is addressing him.

"I just need stitches," says the driller. "Like. Seriously guys. Stitches."

"He's probably wanted for assault," says Carl.

"Jesus." I lay my head on the steering wheel, feeling as though my stomach is being pulled out through my navel. "We're not assholes," I say. I look to my brother for confirmation. I need his flat calming attitude that annoys everyone else. They think his calm suggests a dangerous detachment. But people don't understand Steve. He just turns the wrong things again and again in his head, like a gyroscope.

"A hospital record is a mistake," says Carl. "He's totally high, too."

"Just coke," says the driller.

Steve leans forward to the front seat. "Hospital," he says. "Don't care."

I start the car. "I should know his name."

"Rocky," says the driller.

"Stop being an idiot," says Steve.

"Cody."

I pretend to be Cody's girlfriend, say I found him like this. The intake nurse asks if he has insurance and looks doubtful as Cody searches his wallet. While Steve and Carl wait it out at the wonderful Shoney's, I hunker down in a molded-plastic chair and watch a wiggy-haired evangelist rail from the bolted TV. I'm kind of clutching my brother's bloody hat.

I had been the one to catch Steve with my father's gun after they found Melissa. He was crouched by Dad's workbench, shaking and crying, holding a Smith's T-shirt she'd given him. I couldn't hug him, because getting close was always difficult. We got drunk in my Grandma's old Buick in the garage, and he said he loved Melissa. But his quivering voice made my hair stand on end, and at the funeral, I told my parents he needed help.

After forty stitches, I take Cody home. Through the breath-fogged windows, I watch him lurch from the truck. He stumbles the length of converted boxcars. The street is icy, standing sheets, mirrored by headlights. He looks like a hitchhiker with no place to go.

The next day, as usual, I'm at Shoney's. Steve comes to ask for Randy's money. We don't talk about the night before. Instead, we argue over which of us is greedier for staying in North Dakota to earn a paycheck. It's ugly, and I cry fat ugly tears in the bathroom. It's not like we never fight, but I am shaking when I leave Shoney's.

As I drive through a boxcar village, I have to swerve to miss a coyote. He trots, head down, panting like he is sick. Sitting in the road, I think how beautiful this shit is, then recognize how little I understand this state. In the land of hazmat suits, tankers, and exploding gas, he seems near death. I think his sickness has tamed him. For a minute, he reminds me of Steve.

I get back to the trailer and tell Carl. He finally gives me a look that isn't indifferent.

"God. He was probably dehydrated. Disgusting," he says.

"That was my guess," I say.

When we moved here, Carl took us hiking in North Dakota, Wyoming, and Montana. He complained of industry, like the land was an errant partner. These claims seemed ballsy and lacking in self-reflection, considering the man's job. But then, I didn't know Carl that well.

One night, the river tasted metallic. The ceramic filter proved useless, so we spent hours without water. Coming off the trail, we downed Gatorade at the nearest 7-11, all sunburned, lips pruned and white.

Carl has stopped eating his cereal and is leveling a stare. It's time. I wait for the breakup speech. I am tempted to bring it up myself. Seconds pass, and I open my mouth.

"Can you keep a secret?" he says.

"What? I guess."

"I want us to talk to Randy about a business opportunity."

"The guy who told me to walk past the police with money in my pants? The guy who quotes Bible verses?" I took Randy home one time. When he got out of the car, he said, "I pray that out of His glorious riches He may strengthen you with power." The fuck? Walking away, he raised his hand in a peace sign.

"You're living in an evangelical region," says Carl. A fight is brewing. "Stop being closed-minded."

"I'm not closed-minded. I just hate fanatics."

Carl rolls his eyes, opens a beer, and hands it to me.

He sits beside me, his nearness making me shiver. It's been a long time.

"You mean you want to bet on fights or something, like the other night?"

"If there's a few of us working on it together." He shrugs his shoulders.

"Oh. I get it. Did you talk to my brother about this already?"

"He's only half in the loop," says Carl.

"In the loop." I roll my eyes.

He got up. "God. You're always on me." He walks up to the front of the camper and grabs his computer like he's going to fire up Netflix.

"All right, let's go talk to this guy. But I want Steve to know what's happening."

"Of course," says Carl.

Darcy's is a repurposed Jo-Ann Fabrics, painted ceiling-to-floor in black glitter. Neon bulbs light the corners like ghostly fissures in rock. The paint color alone can give someone clinical depression.

This is the place to do business, though. I've been asked to strip, pole dance, and join a prostitution ring in an old laser tag facility. Promised yearly salary—$100K. "No judgment, but I have a job," I always say.

Tonight, Darcy's is packed. There is one single couple slow dancing, but it looks more like she supports his drunken weight. I peek at her face as I pass, make sure she is OK. Habit. Eyes closed, she appears ambivalent, so I keep walking.

Steve stands at a high-top sipping a Coors. "Randy's

not even here," he says. He looks straight at me. "I don't know what you think you're doing."

"Same as you."

Steve's competitive tone makes me want to punch him. He did this on family ski trips, chased me down black diamond runs when he should have stayed on blue. I feel guilty, like my presence pulls Steve to make bad decisions. Maybe we are too close.

"We're not attached at the hip," I tell him.

It hits the mark. He leans over and whispers something to Carl. Then he turns his back to me, which is chilling.

I leave them and walk toward the bar, pushing through a sweaty pack of drillers. Cody, his nose wrapped in a thick cocoon of gauze, is pouring an Icehouse from the tap. He must have just started here. We make eye contact and he smiles. I order a shot.

"You get sick of the men here?" he asks. He is looking at our table. Maybe he is trying to figure out if Carl and I are together.

"Some are better than others."

"Some people are better than others," he says.

"True."

"Still. It's gotta be tough," he slides me an extra shot, looking around for his boss.

I take it. "It is," I say. "Thanks."

He downs his shot and sweeps the glasses away. I wonder if he has something more to tell me, but I blow off the thought. It's too much to deal with.

At the table, Carl and Steve have decided to talk to Randy at his trailer in Trenton. They're already standing to leave and slipping into winter jackets. Cody shoots me a warning look from the bar, and it makes my hair stand on end, but I keep going. Steve may not know the danger he's in, and I'm all about protecting him, whether he wants it or not.

Randy's trailer sits in a stand of straggling trees flocked with snow, at the edge of a septic looking pond. Rusted out, its deep brown paneling harkens to the 1980s, windows covered in newspaper and a plastic flag in a snow-covered flower pot at the door.

I stop the car. "You know this is how people get abducted and motherfucking killed." I say it to both of them.

I turn back to Steve, but he is scrunched in his seat, one solid line creasing his forehead, as he does when he thinks of something darker.

"Well, c'mon." Carl gets out and starts toward the trailer.

In the yard, a chapped-pink child swings on an old tire in a mismatch of loose winter clothing. She says, "Watch out for that hole in the yard."

Terrifying, I think.

We walk through the snow, skirting a six-foot pit filled with black soot, soil, and rock. Carl tries to put his arm around me, but I shrug him away. The kid wasn't kidding.

Behind the trailer, Randy stands over the rising flames in a rusted-out barrel. He's working, throwing a sock, another sock, a shirt into the flames. He stoops and picks up a dirty blanket. "So you guys want to help with more fights?" he asks.

"Yeah. She's a bookkeeper," says Carl.

The hair prickles. I never felt so shady about being a bookkeeper. It's normally a dorky job. Now I remember the thrill of passing the police with money in my jeans.

Randy says, "Well. I got to get my second-born some fish sticks." He starts toward the front yard. "It's time to eat," he yells.

"I'm not done swinging!"

"Fifth commandment!" he shouts.

The kid runs toward the front door.

"OK. Then let's head out in a sec," says Randy. He closes the door, leaves us in the snow.

If we are going to talk about betting, why do we need a second location? I shuffle my feet in the snow and summon the nerve to say it. "This feels off."

"You always say that about Quiverfulls," says Carl. But he too looks nervous, his face a series of lines. He blows into his hands, rubs them together.

"Did you see his knuckles?" I say. "He's busted the hell out of them."

We all stand close, as in a herd mentality, fostering that false security. But it soon ends. Steve is going from lukewarm to distant. He's watching the door.

"We don't have to be involved just because of that first night," I say.

"Don't say that to him. He's not the kind of person you say that to," says Carl.

"Carl. Who is your friend here?" I thought he had my back. But here is the reality of this place: the rented backhoe, the shovel, the remnants of burned chunks in that pit. I hate to admit I'm scared. I wonder if I'm overthinking it. Carl and Steve don't make eye contact.

"Does Randy know anything about that driller?"

Carl shushes me as the trailer door opens.

"Who's riding with me?" says Randy.

Despite my nausea, I follow Randy's white, windowless van, a kill-mobile reminiscent of horror films. Steve is unusually silent. He actually turns on the radio to some crap classic rock station playing Led Zeppelin and cracks the window to smoke. I finally shout "Hey. Dude. What the hell are we doing?" My throat is tight, and I fight the urge to cry.

"We're going to one of those recreation centers by the lake," says Steve. He flips his ash out the window crack.

I try to navigate the deep plains drifting while not losing my shit.

"Do you know this for sure?"

"No."

"The hell, Steve? What's the matter with you?"

"Nothing."

"Wait. Do you know what happened to that driller? Was it a fight?"

He doesn't answer, so I stop in the middle of the road, fishtailing until the back tires hit a drift. We both seem surprised by the vibration of the car over the wind-perforated snow. The back-end thumps against a drift. I slam it in park.

"Dude. You have to follow them," says Steve.

"Do you know?" I shout at him.

"I don't know," he shouts. "C'mon."

"Why are you lying?"

"Allie, don't piss this guy off."

Headlights grow bright behind us. A twenty-year old Chevy stripped to primer pulls up. It honks so loudly, so insistently it makes my skin crawl.

Steve looks back at the Chevy and shakes his head. "Leave me here. I'm not going to get mad."

"I'm not leaving you here," I say. I put the car in drive. The tires spin for a few seconds, but I rock it from the rut. I feel relieved with solid ground under our wheels. But my brother is getting agitated, looking behind us, checking his phone. This is the same guy who rappelled with me, taught ropes class, set all the anchors. If I touch him, it looks like he will fly apart.

We drive for a mile when his phone buzzes. "Allie, there's a motel up ahead. Just leave me there. They'll come get me."

I pull into the parking lot of a deserted Daylight Inn. The A-line roof is half-caved in on one side, the orange trim peeling. I stare at a plastic deer family sitting askew in snow. The front door is propped open with a liquor bottle.

I don't think he will stay here, but he opens the car door. He isn't afraid of tweakers or squatters. He has the flattest expression. He's not afraid of anything. "Honestly, I'm scared," I say.

"It's OK." But he says it like we are kids, and it isn't.

"Steve. If you can't say what happened, be honest by saying something else—tell me something about that day."

"What day?"

"If you can't tell me straight out about the driller. Say something about how Melissa died."

"Are you fucking kidding?" he says.

"Say some shit that's been hard for you." I just wanted to be assured it was still him.

He sighs, buttons his coat. "We're not kids," he says. He opens the door. "And Carl is not a good person."

I already know it. I had been waiting for Carl to break up when I need to do it.

Steve walks to the open hotel door, looks in the window, and steps inside. If he is worried about tweakers, it doesn't show.

I turn around in the snow and gun it. I clear my stuff out of the Rambler and can't resist leaving Carl the note—"It wasn't so bad."

An hour on the road, I get a text from Steve—her foot was still in her boot. That was worse than anything.

Then, I start crying. I cry for two hundred miles thinking of Melissa's body undetected in the mountains for months. I think of the driller. I drive across the plains, past the billboards, with their admonishments, their promises of retribution, all that bullshit. I am thinking only of my family, how maybe they turned out bad, how maybe I don't know them. Maybe I never did.

GO HOME

Phil lived with his parents, and after smoking a bowl, we floated on deflating air mats in their leafy pool while they scoured the antique mall in Calcutta. A DiGiorno was in the oven, and my mom's Xanax was softening the pot. Still, I felt anxious from my mono and wanted to go inside.

I caressed the hollow of my stomach, enjoying the feel of my own skin. His dog, Snickers, lunged at the screen door with explosive barks.

I had tried entertaining Phil by mocking a coworker's idiosyncratic behavior with a really solid *Seinfeld* impression. In my hometown, I was outgoing and liked trash-talking people, but at college I spent whole days alone in my dorm. Phil never watched Seinfeld, so my joke bombed, and I ended up pulling on his swimsuit strings until he said stop.

Phil lived in the past. He spent hours watching Jonny Quest cartoons while his mother did his laundry. But I'd found out last week he liked ass play, which made him brave about his body, in my opinion.

A frenzied Snickers began chewing the screen. "Don't you think you should feed the dog?" I asked.

"Mom's got it."

"Oh," I said. "Want to go inside and have sex then?"

"Can you not talk for a while? My high." Once Phil pinned me in a bathroom, so it wasn't like we didn't experiment with sadistic stuff.

"I guess so," I said. "Yeah, probably. Hey. Do you hate Tom? I mean, do you want to punch him until he shuts up?" Tom was our boss, and I knew this would start a conversation.

"Not really."

"Yeah. Me, either." I continued tracing the half-moon jut of my hip bone, wondering how long I would feel this horny.

In the dampness, I finished a cigarette on the power plant's catwalk and gazed up several stories at the rolling clouds while thinking of Phil, who hadn't shown for work. A few minutes passed as I watched that flue gas fatten and drift away. I dropped the cherry, aiming for the employee picnic table below, when he burst through the steel door looking like crap. "I got fired," he said.

"They just fucking hired you full time." I removed my hard hat to minimize any flattening of my hair. I still gave a shit, despite a large respirator around my neck, and a nose filled with soot.

"Yeah. I have no idea why."

I knew why. Yesterday, Phil spent an afternoon rescuing a two-foot snapping turtle which had crawled to the parking lot. He failed out of forestry school and seemed conflicted about it. I hadn't decided if I'd go back to college, so we had that in common. Phil spent each day incredibly high, and he wouldn't learn any new skill beyond MIG welding, no matter what Tom asked. Yet he bragged to his friends about this job.

"I can go back to cleaning."

"Sacred Heart? No."

"It paid good money." He changed the subject. "Want to make out?"

"Of course," I said. We had sex in his truck once, but never slutted it up inside the building, though we were once assigned to clean the supply room all day.

Phil suggested walking back separately, because he worried I'd get canned too, but I wouldn't get canned. In two weeks, I'd welded and ground pipe fittings in half the time of the other temps. I reminded these guys of a spunky high school lay, or the girlfriend who put up with their pranks, like filling my hard hat with water. I drank vending machine coffee without complaint and nodded during Tom's long-winded stories about his two passions: his college-age son and biplanes.

"You can see all Coshocton County," Tom said. "You can even see the rubber plant dumping shit into the Walhonding."

"Uh-huh." It's not like Tom would tell his cop brother or call the city, because he could only bitch about "the wasteland" that was Tyndall.

The guys outside our team were creeps. They frequently gave a thumbs-up to my boobs. Once someone grabbed my ass when I bent down at the vending machine. One temp said "I like college girls" ten times in a serial-killer voice until Larry told him to grow up. Larry's patronizing tone made me miss college, but the whole thing didn't seem worth a written complaint.

My mom got me the job through her company We Temp! I couldn't burden her with a new assignment. She was having a meltdown over her second divorce, and the house had become a soundtrack of quietly opening and closing cabinet doors.

Overall, my team of senior journeymen were cool. They'd been shown diversity videos and had daughters.

Phil said, "That's just on the surface. They're really assholes about women."

He said this because our coworker, Larry, commented on the loose tie of my peasant shirt when Phil and I returned from his truck. Larry was hard to hate. Six-foot-five and maybe one hundred sixty, he brought everyone his wife's peanut butter squares, which we had to eat in the break area because of the filth.

What Larry said was, "You can do better than that numb nut."

I liked being perceived as better than Phil, especially when he ignored me to play Magic or hunt deer. We went to high school together, and people liked him. Still, I felt I was slumming it, and the realization brought both a jolt of pity and sexual excitement.

Phil's friend Craig let everyone smoke at his parents' while he unloaded two kilos over the summer. Phil's friends all attended forestry school, played D&D all night, composted, designed bomb shelters, and survived a blizzard in the Appalachians with the "right gear." In high school, they were known as smart, reclusive potheads. I knew them to cultivate misanthropy.

Attending college didn't make them open-minded, either. Everyone we knew scattered across Ohio. Colleges were as plentiful and diverse as bars. I went to a Bible-thumping university and attended mandatory chapel, and my best friends went to a hippie college in southern Ohio where they did internships in goat herding and got edible condoms at mixers.

Forestry reinforced the guys' hatred for Reagan, who'd opened oil leases on wilderness land while refusing to limit trade so that southern Ohio was a ghost town of steel plants and middle Ohio was a boom of strip mining. They also hated Clinton. Craig's politics were the most fickle, and since he was the Dungeon Master with weed, no one pushed him. He was the king of dickish insults and he controlled the stereo with the Spin Doctors and the Grateful Dead.

His girlfriend Megan was a dick, too, and together they bugged everyone. While the guys mostly rolled with Craig, Megan's contrariness enraged them, and their toxic hatred turned to low blows about her skinniness. I hated being the only other woman. They didn't totally want us around, but felt insecure without us.

"Try not stroking Phil's ego all the time. It's gross," said Megan, as she gently closed the door to Craig's kitchen. She smelled of patchouli and cigarettes and carried a giant patched-leather hobo purse, which she unzipped.

Not that I cared what anyone thought of my relationships, but I didn't like being bossed. "Whatever, dude. Everyone knows you're down on Craig everytime you go for something in his van."

"I don't want to fight," she said. She pulled out a copy of *Atlas Shrugged* and a tape by Ani DiFranco and held them out. "Here. Both are enlightening."

"OK," I said. "Everyone I know hates this book."

"I'm sure they don't get it."

"Oh. Yeah. I'll tell them that."

"We should hang out sometime. I'm sure you're starving for conversation." She rolled her eyes Phil's direction.

"Why me? You have other friends."

"Why not? We got to watch our backs." She slung her ugly bag over her shoulder and walked into the other room.

I resented the assumption we had to forge an inevitable friendship because we were women, so in Phil's truck, I drew my feet up on his seat, remained silent, and watched as we floated by the Super 8, rusted oil derricks, and those outbuildings families used both for lawn equipment and parties.

Phil stewed over one of Craig's gender critiques regarding his clothes, which I hadn't heard because I was in the bathroom peeing and flipping through *Playboy*. Next thing I knew we were out in the truck, Phil breathing hard, in full panic attack, as he slapped the steering wheel.

"Chill out," I said and lit a cigarette without rolling down the window.

"I need to drop you. I want to go to Rivercrest for a drink by myself."

"You mean you want to break up?" At that moment,

I needed reassurance because we were in a bad way.

"Yes." But, it came out tentative.

Back rigid, I pulled in my knees, my throat closing as tears started. He cranked the stereo to cover my crying. Maybe it was my mom or missing school, or maybe I was embarrassed at the prospect of him dumping me, but I curled into a fetal position in the passenger's seat.

"Oh, for God's sake stop acting like a four-year-old." He turned down Nine Inch Nails.

"Fuck you."

"Oh, nice. Fuck you."

We drove another two miles to his house in silence.

"Well. Here's your car," he said.

I opened the door and half fell out, my legs numbed.

"Hey. I hadn't meant to break up," he yelled

I unlocked my car and threw my drunk-high body against the driver's seat.

"Are you OK to drive?"

Like he cared? I tore off, spraying grass and hunks of dirt, forcing him to deal with his mom later.

God knows why Phil's bedroom was dark for three days, only their family room was lit when I drove past, but it stressed me out. I finally caught him at the Citgo. He'd parked by the propane tanks where high school students paid scrubs to buy beer.

Phil started when he saw me, but walked to my window. "I don't know why you keep calling me."

His self-congratulatory tone irritated me. "I hear you are dating that girl who sells coke. As your friend, I just want you to know you can do better."

"I appreciate that," he said. "I do."

"My mom can get you a job, and not as a janitor."

"I do hate my job," he said. "Father Ferren is a ballbuster."

Phil never realized how unintentionally problematic his comments were. "Yeah. Well. I think you could do better," I said.

"Sure. Let me know what she says." He leaned down into the window. "Listen, you better not fuck with Vi. Her family can put the hurt on."

"What does that mean?"

"It means they take their name and revenge seriously. I'm a guy and she scares me." He looked around the gas station, as if this secret knowledge thrilled him and, by proxy, me. Leaned close, I smelled the mouth he'd decided to stop brushing.

I rolled my eyes, but couldn't resist asking, "Want to hang out?"

He stood and stretched. "No can do. Got plans with my girlfriend. Maybe some other time, though."

"Like later this week," I said.

"Sure. Later this week. Let me know about your Mom. Gotta get going."

"OK. See you." I said it to his back.

Several guys at work invited me shooting in the strip pits, but when I arrived it was just Larry and Tom and some dudes I didn't know. They pulled gun bags and coolers from their vans.

We set up beside a yellowish creek littered with spent cans. A graffitied boulder read *Jim Morrison is Alive*— as if anyone gave a shit. I hadn't known what to wear, so I threw on my college sweatshirt and homemade jean shorts.

Tom pointed to my flip-flops. "Watch out for snakes," he said.

"Har har." I still smiled.

Tom's friends ignored us, so for an hour we set Budweiser cans on the Morrison boulder and shot them with a .22, Tom helping me line the sights. One of Tom's friends had an SKS, and he probably thought it would be funny to see me shoot it.

"Is this for deer?" I asked.

"Only if you are mad as hell at that deer." They laughed.

One guy said, "Hit that can square."

I hefted the gun to my shoulder, uncomfortable with its unwieldiness.

"You can keep pulling."

As I shot, my throat tightened with anxiety. Bullets ricocheted off the rock and exploded small clouds of dust. I envisioned bloody injuries, glassy eyes, and paramedics. I couldn't imagine this did much more than cathect some pent rage. It seemed stupid. They laughed until Tom gave them a look.

"Here, I'll take that off your hands," said one guy.

Humiliated, I handed it back, and adjusted my jean shorts, which had ridden up my crotch.

As the sun disappeared, they shot less and drank more, pulling old nylon camp chairs out of one guy's van. I downed three Rolling Rocks and listened to them shit-talk the world, echoing their criticisms like we'd always hung out. I smiled so much my face ached, but I didn't like them.

After six beers, they got around to talking about

Phil. Larry said, "He's fucked up. He was a bad hire. He was a loser." They said he was trashy, but what did that mean? I didn't mention Phil wore the same Meat Puppets shirt every time we met up, and his teeth often bled when we kissed.

"He was just unemployment waiting to happen." Sunken into his camp chair, Larry was all belly.

"It's sad how lazy he is," said Tom.

"And weird. He probably jerked off in the bathroom," said Larry. Tom's friends laugh, but not Tom.

"I got to go," I said.

At my car, Tom leaned to the window, so I rolled it down. "Don't take any of these guys seriously."

"At this point, that's my motto."

"You're a good girl, Charlie Brown."

In some ways, I didn't mind him talking to me like I was nine. There was zero sexuality in his stance, though his hairy hands remained on my car door. Unlike other men at the plant he wasn't acting gross. And the guys at college just tried to load me up with drinks.

"Don't go finding Phil tonight."

"I won't," I said.

I was riding Phil in the passenger's seat of his truck outside the bar, Cat Ballou's, bracing myself with my elbow against the window, when I realized I could proposition someone without feeling like a slut. Inside, I'd been chatting with the bartender, when I saw Phil walk in and try to sell his seedy dime bags to a sunken-faced guy by the door. I walked past him, stopped, whispered "Wanna screw?"

"Sure," he said.

I felt really fucking strong.

Phil leaned over and kissed me hard. A fleck of blood dotted his lip. He whispered. "My girlfriend is showing up later."

"Are you telling me to clear out?"

"I'm saying I'm going back in there alone," he said. "For your own safety."

"Give me a break." I lit a cigarette without rolling down the window.

"Seriously, I'm going in," he said.

The walk to my car, I felt washed-out and sore, unsnapped bodysuit scraping my thigh. Through the windshield, I watched a couple girls cross the street from Red Head, their hair huge, their jeans tight and shiny.

Maybe that was her. I told myself it was better I'd had sex with him first. But that didn't help, since he'd seemed a mess—selling her dime bags, throwing his life away. Completely still, I watched them walk the entire way into Cat Ballou's.

Rivercrest Lounge was a hangout for the oldest locals and a super club for fish fries, but in high school it was known as the "drug bar." Two seventeen-year-old punk girls with safety pins in their noses had made a rep for drinking Schnapps in a back booth after letting an old man feel them up, and the place became a symbol for what you should and shouldn't do in the town. But I'd been in here my first week home from school, and it just felt like a dive where you ate fried food and talked about work.

Parked beside Phil's truck, Megan leaned too close offering me a one-hitter, and I wondered if I invited people to disregard my comfort.

"Supposedly, his girlfriend cuts people, you know."

"Maybe I shouldn't go in."

"Do whatever makes you feel good, but I don't think he's worth it."

"Uh."

She rolled her eyes, and zipped the hobo bag. "I'm going across the street to the Dollar Store. You let me know how this turns out."

"Maybe I'm stupid."

"Hey, I'm not judging. Just come get me if you need me." Megan loved to flex her open-minded muscles. When she was really high, she once explained the difference between sympathy and empathy. I let her go on because I was lonely.

Rivercrest wasn't like Cat Ballou's. Windowless, it smelled of bleach, and the eight-foot ceiling made it feel like a basement. The jukebox pumped out Genesis. I tried to project a don't-fuck-with-me vibe, but everywhere I looked, men stared.

His boots propped on the chair across from him, Phil stretched the width of a corner table laughing with guys I'd never met. I saw him first and walked to his table. "How's it going?" I said.

"You should not be here," he said.

"Why?" Maybe he wouldn't be in the frame of mind to hear my take on what people were saying. But I could save him from his lazy fear of change. He could pick another college, stop wearing the damn oil-stained jean jacket and quit eating the same frozen pizzas and watching the same cartoon marathons on his parents' TV.

"I'm just going to have a drink." I eased into the ripped vinyl booth.

"That seat's taken," he said.

Around the table, the guys stopped talking, yet pretended not to notice me. One laughed.

"Seriously?" I asked. My eyes burned.

"Yeah. This is the only time her old man isn't around. Scoot."

"Jesus. She's married?"

"She's talking about me again, isn't she?" Beside me, Vi stood in the dim red glow, thin and sinewy in a white tank and blue leather jacket, hair wild. She sent a tingle through me. "What's your problem, anyway?"

"Nothing. Sorry. I just came here to see Phil."

"Well. You've seen him."

We had something in common, and she needed to understand that. "Yeah. I wanted to tell him about the job my mom lined up."

"I thought you guys were just friends."

"Well," I said.

Vi's friend or sister with a faux hawk and pink swaths of eyeshadow over lid slid up behind her. She looked far less reasonable, and I could see where they were coming from. I didn't belong, and I had been talking shit. I felt a mono headache starting. Why did acting in my own self-interest have to end badly? In college, I walked home alone, passed out in male friends' beds, drank to obvious excess, isolated myself from well-meaning friends, ate horribly. Despite these displays of indifference, I never completely felt at ease.

Maybe there wasn't a convenient time to assert myself. Clearly, Vi fed off challenge. I bet she never whined.

I felt the flat-palm slap, a bright sting spreading from my cheek, bone to my teeth.

"Hey, man, that was totally unnecessary." I knew better than to fully stand and considered how I might walk to my car safely with my head down. Phil was laughing.

I wanted to say we should cut each other slack. He was nothing to get upset over. Really, I was the asshole.

Armed with Red Head coffee and chocolate donuts, I drove to work and used my car mirror to load L'Oréal foundation over the small circles of blue fingerprints darkening on my cheek.

Tom was quiet the entire time I shadowed him to the tool check. We were replacing spent grinding wheels, when he said, "What happened to you?"

"It was my fault."

"The hell you say? Did she get the best of you?"

"I was in the wrong place."

"I bet."

He wouldn't resume working until I spilled everything. I unloaded and cried. Tom never liked Phil, and he listened intently to a description of Vi selling cocaine. He told me to use vinegar on the bruises, though I'd smell like a "goddamn salad." When we hugged, I pressed my face into his shoulder and felt safe.

"I haven't fought since I was nineteen," he said.

"I'm not nineteen."

"I'm not busting your balls. It's just not becoming."

"I really hate that word," I said.

My last week, I worked less, and Tom said nothing. The forest rangers had gone back to Hocking Tech, so I stayed home reading novels assigned in my single literature class.

I drove by Phil's once to see him watering his parents' lawn. He might have looked up.

I returned Megan's book before a show at the Night Owl in Columbus where her friends' punk band Squeal Like You Mean It opened for Cracked Headlight. Sweaty and elated, she and Craig and I danced to New Wave until we had sore, whiplashed necks. We planned a hiking trip to Utah. We trash-talked Phil—his taste in partners, his intelligence, his looks.

Craig said, "You look better without him. Less sick."

"Mono is gone." But I struggled with headaches, so maybe it wasn't. Elastica played and the Night Owl screened *Supervixens* so the flash of peach skin, lips, and straining leather seared into my brain. I soaked in each detail, exhaling slow breaths.

"Hey. Phil's girlfriend is on her way to prison, by the way," said Craig.

They told me Vi got picked up at the traffic light in front of Giant Eagle carrying an ounce of coke and her kid riding without a carseat. "It was only a matter of time because there was always a cop driving by her house," said Craig. "She got three years. What a piece of shit."

I already knew. Tom had called his cop brother. I guess he thought of himself as a kind of father figure, and that disturbed me. I wasn't a coworker, an equal, but a daughter to guide and instruct. Gross.

"Pretty shitty if you have a kid," said Megan.

"Yeah." Saying it didn't feel right. I suddenly hoped Craig and Megan would break up. They could be such assholes. Eventually, they would find work as rangers in a national park. Their Facebook pic would show five khaki-clad hikers with arms slung over each other like it was a camping supply ad.

"What's wrong with you?" said Megan.

"I'm not feeling good," I said.

They didn't believe me, but at the time I thought I sold it. My lack of introspection made me tone deaf to social cues, so maybe they even knew I was involved in Vi's arrest, however indirectly. It seemed best to leave. "Actually, I'm feeling like an asshole." I pulled my bag over my shoulder.

"Why should you feel bad?" said Megan. "She's the drug addict"

I pushed my way toward the door.

"Well, whatever. Give me a call," she yelled.

In the street, five drunk dudes rocked a car to their football chants. I took a side alley, wanting to prove I could take care of myself, become something more complete, whatever that meant. I didn't know. Maybe I should have looked over my shoulder to see if they followed. But if I wasn't self-sufficient then, when would I be?

BOTTLE ROCKETS

"I've watched *Invasion of the Body Snatchers* sixteen times," says Jon as I knead his back. "Does that mean something?"

I don't answer but skim his spine's notches. I'm a terrible masseuse, but he asked for a backrub, so he's getting a dangerously bad one.

"Sci-fi movies are a turn on," he says.

"I believe it," I say—in that, I believe they turn him on. Last week we visited his parents, and in their basement he wanted to make out during *Aliens*, groping during flashing images of one terrifying puppet, just after we'd eaten a robust turkey dinner. He was also undeterred by Alex Trebek loudly posing answers as upstairs his parents watched their favorite show. "What is Madagascar," says Jon. We keep making out. It definitely says something about him, but it isn't something bad.

Jon prefers bodily invasion, Hollywood cashing in on people's collective nervousness about being consumed: *The Thing, Aliens, V, Breeders*. We don't have this in common, but the last ten months have been good. I've been less of a hypochondriac, felt less raw and guarded during nights out. And I barely think about mortality, which seems healthier. Still, I only have a single drawer in Jon's apartment, where my underwear lay in a small pile.

We finish nectars, salt-spiked umami cakes, sunken on a couch under a bay window in sunlight where our thighs still touch as we eat. With other partners, I have ridden bikes through windy corridors and blinding cliffs of high rises. Virtually sedentary, Jon and I eat salty, oily snacks, creamy food from deep bowls, adding thick adipose layers. Still, despite this, my body plummets to triage-worthy temps in the winter, and I make Jon bear the burden of shoveling. In the snow, he howls from the porch.

He knocks on the window, a warped icicle gripped like a snow cone fashioned of crooked bone, droplets clinging to mitten's weave, his nose coppery with aggravated Rosacea. He gestures, runs around the porch, slips but recovers, and returns to taunt me with his shovel.

He went to school for film, but now helps narcissistic jack-offs sell medical supplies, mainly needles. There's a hideous abstract sculpture in his building's lobby, a genderless person befriending a needle, but it looks more like the figure has taken a Jesus-spike through the hand. I don't like to visit him. There are too many actual needles in the office where he manages spreadsheets: three-edged, filiform, 13-millimeter needles, 130-millimeter needles. They also sell customer information, sometimes to dubious medical companies. This last company they sold to supplied illegal bath salts online. So in addition to feeling badly about the work, he questions me over his own ethics.

He has the least seniority, and in the bathroom, he heard someone refer to him as The Carpet Square. That's a good reason to quit, but also a needle may accidentally enter his eye, stabbing him through the dilated pupil, one smooth pointless shot in the cornea.

"How would this happen?" he says. "Bodily invasions of any kind are rarely accidental."

"Needle-factory brawl," I say. I can obsess over this if he can watch so many movies with elaborate puppetry that gets him off.

"I wish we had more of a medical background." But then I would probably be more phobic. For instance, I have a terrifying mole. It has deepened from shale to nipple-pink, coincidently the color of my urine, and my bowels are giving me trouble, maybe causing the change in my urine. It might be a stretch to think my bowels changed my mole.

As we shovel the sidewalk, Jon returns to a recurring discussion—he wants to replace Buster Keaton, my deceased bulldog. For him, my hypochondria stems from missing my mush-faced dog. Everyone feels their dog is genuinely intuitive, but Buster Keaton got me. When Zooey Deschanel came out with that annoying commercial, Buster Keaton always barked, sharing my irritation, his mouth as frothy and salmon as I felt as he nipped at the screen and at Zooey Deschanel's ukulele-strumming hands. Saturday, Jon again mentions getting a new dog, which at first causes me to balk at the potential destruction of the empty space Buster Keaton has left in the apartment, a space his chew-toys and bristle bones still populate, like a surrealist landscape about dogs as a concept.

That night, in the bathroom, after fondue, my weight is twenty pounds greater, explaining the general softness of my stomach, which now obsesses me so that I run my hands over it in bed, while hoping Jon doesn't think I masturbate with him under the covers. I would wait until he was gone. I had expanded beyond my most expansive point, at eighteen, when my diet was pizza, a year I became what friends would describe as Plasticine. "Plasticine" leaves my mouth as Jon evicts me from the scale. He too has gained twenty-five pounds, and he makes a mewing noise like a wounded snow leopard in a ravine.

If we were basset hounds, the vet would prescribe a special diet like Nutritional Nuggets or Natural Dog, and if we were elephants we would die in a quagmire. In a moment of conflated-ego we both agree: Relationships are all about each other's bodies, beginning with obsession, moving to comfort, finally, the bulking up after post-coital calm. Now he's closer to my way of thinking. My hypochondria doesn't seem so disjointed.

My metabolism has sunken into a glacial period: iced-over explorers slowly traverse my intestines shouting "smoke ahead," their pickaxes driving into a lip of tissue. That's not true. The intestinal travelers are quite silent because it requires so much effort to move through the permafrost of my bladders and veins, a Yakutsk, supplying its diamonds but remaining frozen.

My first breakfast salad is late February, and it prompts Jon to say asparagus and raise one eyebrow, but I remain silent. In my mind I immaturely shout I CANNOT HAVE A BOWEL MOVEMENT, and it reverberates in my pulmonary, intrajugular and diploic veins, but stops short of the intestines frozen beneath my stomach.

"Jon," I say. "Do you want to travel someplace really dorky, but out in the boondocks?"

"A trip?"

"In other words, some place I'm ashamed to say I want to go." Copper Springs' invasive pop-up ads have made me want to get a massage, take the waters, slough off bad skin. I think of this as I drag a dagger icon into my I-hate-Zooey-Deschanel Tumblr. I have made a gif of her barfing small stringed instruments, as an adorable puppy barks at her. I call it "Bark-Barfing," and suddenly realize I'm not good at naming gifs, and it depresses me.

Jon stops stamping a squid on a birthday invitation for his six-year-old niece, Candice, his hand suspended above the squid's immature yet threatening tentacle. Candice loves squid, not knowing squid eek through the water, rotating their hooks that are just the size for boring a hole in a child, an image so disturbing I can't finish my breakfast.

"Where are we going?" he asks, his fingers poised mid-stamp, his mouth a straight line.

"Are you reluctant or tired of that squid?" I honestly can't tell.

"No. I want to go on a dorky trip with all of my muster."

"How much muster? Enough to call you a colonel?"

"You beat me too it!" He said. "No. I Poupon anyone with more muster."

"Love it," I say and deflate onto the shoal of the over-blown cushions, and stare out the window at the elderly couple shuffling down the street. The flip mention of this bodily habit depresses me. The elderly likely can't have bowel movements, either. So much in common. So so much.

We schedule a couple's massage and drive to Michigan, a series of events which seem a little dorky until the throes of the check-in process reveal them to be ridiculous. In matching robes, we read *Dwell* in a waiting room where furniture is positioned at protractor-worthy ninety-degree angles and a wood-burning fireplace spans twenty feet of the room. I'm not even exaggerating, twenty fucking feet. If someone took a photo of us right now, it could be used for *Dwell*.

Birds weave an accompaniment to a quartet of soft pan-flutes, as through the windows, a grayish older man, in a billow of steam, tests the dark waters of a hot tub. His tentative actions suggest a tub filled with flesh-eating virus, and he turns at the last minute, offering a view of his butt through the sixteen-foot windows, mesmerizing me with his body's intricate creases. Through the folds his skin appears long and pliable, closer to loose-fitting pants, yet his buttocks emerge from the slack like an apple. I study his lack of self-consciousness and admire him.

A girl arrives in a vapor of sandalwood, hands us cucumber water, and with non-threatening gestures introduces herself as Zoey, which elicits a sigh. This also brings on a renewed need to relieve myself, and revives the feeling of possessing a marmot in my gut. Imagining the happy colon pictured on the package of Garden of Life not only fails to bring relief; it annoys me.

We swish silently in our robes through low-lit rooms filled with ferns and callas, when a guy dressed in a smock appears, joins Zoey, and introduces himself as Rod. Not even kidding. Rod. It now feels like a sex party, a phrase that elicits the internal berating remark: Cheryl, how about orgy? What's the matter with the precision of that word? Orgy. Orgy? The glowing purple tub engulfed in fake ivy announces sex in healthy, comforting, burning, burning oil. I project the aura of not being weirded out but am weirded out.

Cloying sandalwood does not bring on legitimate relaxation. Home remedies haven't helped, though I am fortified with Garden of Life products: colon cleanses, probiotics, St. John's, psyllium powders. Often I have asked Jon to leave me in productive solitude with excuses like a need for croissants from Sweet Cakes or my sudden concern over carbon monoxide poisoning, the need for detectors from Ace Hardware.

As Rod works under the keen of whales, I imagine he massages everything from me, and wonder if being an agent of expulsion disturbs him. In his oblivion, he hums whale songs. Or it could be Jon. No. Thank God. It's just Rod.

At home, we sing constantly, especially the Magnetic Fields' *69 Love Songs*, which suddenly enters my head and swirls around, to the whales' accelerated moans and clicks. Daily, I sing these songs to Jon, prompting him to make requests. "I'll hear that again," he says. Yet he hates live music, and when we walk two blocks to the Empty Bottle, he buys the earplugs from the bar, under a sign that reads: "Take care of your ears. The band won't."

Once, for me, he stood through a noise band, growing the orange plugs, like giant skin polyps, from his ears, yet smiling. He napped, balanced with one arm bearing fulcrum on his bag, pushing away, as damp bearded dancers swayed around us. He brags he can always be comfortable and is a candidate for apocalypse survival leader, an image eliciting visceral dreams about strength, images of a healthy liver and spleen.

After the massage, amidst a rhythmic popping of overhead racquetballs, Rod and Zoey stare at the oil bath, and following an uncomfortable silence, retreat through the room's bamboo door. This facility doubles as a club. The closing door brings a feeling of nakedness, of me in the center of the court, balls popping me in the hefty stomach.

Jon's half-drunken eyes fluttering, he rests against the hot tub and dozes. He has conquered a recent interview, been hired for a better job, and will no longer be called Carpet Square by a band of Neanderthals selling medical supplies. Earning this, he rests. The seat slopes like the shoals of a baptismal river, and in the purplish glow our skin appears bruised, like we've traveled far, are exhausted and broken. I am reminded of the song "The Big Rock Candy Mountain," where the lakes are a panacea for hobos, with waters of whiskey and stew.

I ask Jon if whiskey and stew comfort him. "I've never had a good stew."

He is serene and naked, his ass jack-knifed toward me. He asks, "Should it be this hot?"

"It depends. Do you mean the water?"

This is our first trip after months when my former roommate made it difficult for us to be alone. She complained of depression, wrapped herself in a three-wolf blanket, and sat on the front porch chain smoking. We lived on Ashland Avenue, and my roommate left the door open. It was an accident, Buster Keaton' death, but I didn't leave the house for weeks. I broke up with Jon; I got back together with him. You can't lock doors or window or control your space, so you're basically screwed with a roommate, and then it's up to you to blame yourself. But if I thought of it as a fluke, I might feel even feel worse.

Jon and I lay in the shallow tub, leaned against each other so we wouldn't go under.

"It's starting to cool down," he says, but I'm not sure what he means.

For minutes, we don't speak.

He says, "Let's adopt one tomorrow. I've wanted a dog. Bloom, Brawny, and Blake are all good names."

"Who names a dog Bloom?" I ask. "Blake is a frat name."

"True."

I'm not going to cry because I'm not at home, but when I mew a little, and someone immediately knocks on the door.

"They think we're having sex," he whispers, and raises his eyebrows.

"Or maybe there's a fire?" I say.

Jon grunts, screams "Yes," and smacks his arm provocatively until I whisper "Jesus! Stop." The door seems thin, and my adrenaline pumps, because whoever is listening hasn't moved. We are all silent, as if in some kind of decency standoff. Finally, the person retreats in a rustle of sheets. "Yeah, I'm sure I know what they're thinking."

"So?" he says.

He sings "The Big Rock Candy Mountain" and I settle on thoughts of hobos getting what they want, and the railroad-men tipping their hats. Much better. "Rod wouldn't tip his hat."

"No way," says Jon. "Rod's a Rod-bag."

"That makes no sense."

Jon says nothing.

One week later, I emerge from the bathroom where I had been tracing constellations of my potentially cancerous moles. They just sit there, in golden-brown treachery. Jon asks me to move in, and then, if I'm cool with it, we could get married. Just like that. And he's holding a plunger as if it just occurred to him.

A few months later, we've rented a house, and Jon has taken to making short movies again. The lights are low in the neighborhood when Jon shoots a long take of a bicycle crash. He has chosen this location for his bicycle-action short, about pod-people who when angry transform into Teletubbies. Murderous Teletubbies. It's half animated, so it actually makes more sense.

It's dusky, someone has a fixie, but the tires on the gravel and the huffing and puffing are only a little nostalgic. Harold Lloyd jumps and barks, his chest hitting my calves. I have to bribe him to be silent with something called a pig-wrap.

Hands on my hips, I watch Jon goad people into semi-believable behavior. I think of how the old hymns ingrained in our psyches are about comfort, escapism, and reward and almost never about enjoying life. I resent my religious background. A friend of ours, on camera, sings a familiar song.

On cue, the pod-tubby leans and lights the bottle rocket, as another person films. The traffic is a solid noise, ticking smoothness, in unbearable heat. A man comes out to water his lawn. Sometimes I feel inexplicably sad, despite being comfortable. Jon is laughing.

I lift my hand to shade my face from the fading sun, and the bottle rocket in a smoky line nicks my pinky, explodes, breaking the pink half-moon tip, singeing it, bringing blood. Later I find out it missed my nose by a centimeter. Jon's face appears above me, still calm. I think it went right through, I say. At least I imagine I say this. Kind of amazing.

THE CALUMET

Liz was parked in an industrial corridor of Gary watching stray dogs dig in the dirt of an abandoned lot. The paper factory chugged a cloud of sulfides, enveloping the houses in the scent of wet wool and cabbage. Liz smoked out of her cracked window despite frozen-white fingers and blue nail beds, an idiot for freezing, waiting, and being conspicuous. She texted her boyfriend—*Get up, douche, or we're done.* She honked. No Rich. She was beginning to wonder if their static was becoming radio silence.

She reached for another cigarette and felt around in her half-zipped duffel bag. There was the reassurance of the thick envelope of cash from the sale of her Toyota. Her mom had padded that payout for sure, because she was a better person than Liz. All her cash in the world, and it was starting to make her paranoid. She slammed on the horn again. A dog barked. Rich's battered front door didn't open.

Of course, Rich was hung over from the Low Down last night, and gun-shy about what they had decided to do to Janet. Honestly, Liz was scared too. They needed to move on this or spend another year in Gary.

She pressed the horn for a full three seconds. Nothing. A cruiser turned the corner, creeping past the factory gate. There were always police in this neighborhood and honking only brought them closer, the equivalent of shark chum. They had to investigate everything. Two forms of job security in this town: cops and crime scene clean-up. The cop passed Liz and looked in the car, a dude with a big mustache, and muttonchops creeping over his cheeks like an illness. She sent Rich the text, *Walk to Victor's, asshole*, and hit the gas before Serpico could turn around.

Rich had been so excited about their plan to cheat Janet; it surprised Liz he was screwing it up. A walking disaster, Janet would sit at the dingy Low Down and openly admit her toddler slept unsupervised a block away. She was ridiculously skinny, bony limbs like a praying mantis. Whenever she did bumps without going to the bathroom, Ronnie, the owner, would tell her, "No drama." Despite having slept with Janet, Ronnie gave her no slack, either. A lot of people in Gary wished the worst on Janet.

"Janet, I wish half your bullshit was true," Rich had said after his fifth shot of Old Crow. He and Janet had gone to high school together. Of course, that's not why he believed her. Rich was always hopeful a scam would pay out. He sat forward on the red vinyl bench listening, his eyelids licking back over ghostlike orbs. He worked his mouth, wanting Janet's alleged stash to be real, with the same anxiety he displayed at any difficult situation, anxiety floating above him, like a Tesla sphere.

It amazed Liz that Janet had been her first friend since leaving New York, and that they'd once spent every night at the Low Down getting wasted. It was the kind of bar where a country band performed behind a cage of chicken wire. The walls were decorated with beer signs. On weekdays, Credence blared like it was 1975, and occasionally there was an Eminem track. Liz wasn't proud of using Janet to unload, as she verbalized the worst of her past. Janet was the kind of girl who took it and was too insecure to say no.

In turn, Janet drilled out tales about her movie "star" granddad, Dick Jarmen, who was an extra on *Bonanza* for three seasons, gave up and returned home to collect Medicaid. She bullshitted with anyone in earshot. People grew weary of it and moved tables. Ronnie pretended he didn't know her. But everyone around here had a brush-with-fame story.

Last night, Rich and his friend Derek listened to Janet's bullshit about a mountain of meth worth seventy-five thousand, enough to get anyone out of Gary. Derek was one of those friends Liz hung out with, the one friend left over from Rich's "less than above-board" days. Together, Rich and Derek had tried so many marginal activities—a little bit of insurance fraud, a car scam he didn't really explain, and skimming credit cards at Gas Depot.

Lately, Derek worked at one of the clean-up companies, Clean City, and had done a meth job until 6 a.m. A fucking bear trap had been hidden under some blankets. A crew member walked right into it. "Sliced to the ankle bone," Derek had said. They got off early. He'd been resting his head on the back of the booth, motionless for a half-hour, like the taxidermied elk above him. But when Janet said three pounds, Derek sat up as if someone were already throwing free money through the bar. "We could sell it for you," he said.

"I dunno. It's going to be shit anyway," said Rich. But he was already getting that vulnerable-yet-crazy look where money was concerned. When he and Derek talked money, they grew desperate, words gathering in a power source with the potential to light a city, creating their own grid. They could pull it from nowhere.

"It's good stuff," said Janet.

"Why would a guy with that much product hang out with you, anyway?" said Rich.

Janet was leaned back so that her hair was tinged blue by the flickering neon Milwaukee's Best sign inches above her. "He just likes what I give him, man," she said.

"Janet, you pick the worst guys. You can't see shit in the opposite sex. I told you that in high school," said Rich.

"I'm not really into him. I'm waiting around to take his shit, because he hit my kid and all."

"Rich, none of this is true," said Liz.

"I've known Janet a long time," said Rich. "She doesn't lie when it counts."

"That's exactly when she lies," said Liz.

Liz's real hatred for Janet could be summed up in one incident. Last summer, Janet left her three-year-old, Destiny, in a car for five hours, windows rolled up, ninety-degree heat. The kid's lips were a dry, puckered crater in her face, and even in the hospital, she wouldn't drink for hours. They hooked an IV to the kid, who was one giant blister in the white hospital sheets.

"I'm no skank, like you, Liz," said Janet. "I didn't have no three-way with these dudes. That's why I can't be friends with a person like you. Sorry."

Liz rolled her eyes. "Janet. Shut up."

Janet, eyes still on Liz, opened her purse slightly and aimed it toward the table revealing a Ziploc of meth—800 labs shut down, and the stuff still floated around in the coffee shops, the rest stops of Gary.

Rich had barely let his eyes flit down, but he was looking. "See babe. I told you she didn't lie about important stuff."

"I just can't find anyone to buy it," said Janet.

"I know people," said Derek before he started laughing, a deep rumble like the sound of a freight truck passing.

That's when Ronnie had turned up the music and given them the get-the-fuck-out look. Rich and Derek had grown jumpy. Of course, Rich took it for granted that Liz would produce the twenty percent to get Janice to part with her stash. Talking a mile a minute, they made an arrangement for the consignment situation, Liz's small nest egg up front, and the rest of the proceeds down the line. They'd meet at Victor's the next night and make a trade. They were gulping the last of their beers when Ronnie kicked them out.

By the time she hit the highway towards Victor's, Liz was pissed as hell at Rich for sleeping away his hangover. She would have to stall Janet while Rich dragged his ass out of bed. So much for them coordinating shit. She reached over to the passenger's seat and opened her duffel again to recheck it. She had clothes, shampoo, weed, a toothbrush, and *The Talented Mr. Ripley*, the last book she'd read for college, back when she was still an environmental studies major, floating to class,

AMANDA MARBAIS

buffeted safely on a river of students. She ran out of
money, and she didn't want to be a hundred grand in
debt. Something more immediate was needed. Before
driving to Rich's, she'd spent the morning packing
at her one room-rental while her landlady, a single
woman named Ms. Turley, cranked the Lifetime TV
movie downstairs, feeding two retrievers Cheetos and
shouting commands.

Rich had said, "Once we get the whole seventy-five,
let's crash at your mom's in Chicago." But when they
got to Chicago, she wouldn't stop home. She'd see her
mother when things improved. To witness the worry
Rich would inspire in her mother would be too much.

Liz felt burned out from the last year. Whatever
she had done, she didn't want to get caught or fucked
over. She pulled her grandma's hand-me-down Buick
into a Citgo and parked under the glow of an orange
light. Everything from the stacked tires to the white
smoke pluming from the smokestacks drove her nuts.
She put her head on the steering wheel, in dread over
her shit decisions.

When she lifted her head, a guy pumping gas was
staring. His kid in the backseat looked up from his
iPad and stared, too. Hands shaking, she opened the
envelope, fifteen thousand deep—three months of tips,
the Toyota money, plus some extra Mom slipped in just
because. She wondered again how her mother could be
so much better than her.

Some dude walked past on his way to the highway
and turned toward the car. "Keep walking," said Liz.
She would have run him over for half this money. He
kept walking.

What to do with the seventy-five? Rich hadn't been right since he lost his dad. Rich and his dad had been on a hundred hunting trips, Indiana's pastime. Liz thought the 12-gauge in the face was intentional. She'd never tell Rich that, since he'd found his dad still harnessed to the tree stand. In a way she wasn't good for Rich, since she couldn't reach in and find any strength, any genuine sympathy any more.

She pulled two thousand—a little insurance—from the envelope, rolled it in a pair of underwear and wedged it in the metal supports under the seat. Rich complained of her glibness and insincerity over his dad's death once he began a cocktail of olanzapine and Depakote, which gave him a brief calm. She decided to go back to Chicago. But when she was leaving, he freaked out, folded like a paper-doll in their kitchen, split his lip from the fall, and she held his face between her hands, and watched his chest rise and fall, blue eyes focusing and receding. He went from sadistic and strong to being reminiscent of a tagged deer, with his sharp features and pale brown hair, blood trickling over one blank eye. She took care of him for days, kept him from sleeping in his car when paranoia drove him to find a safe space.

For someone living in a city where the drinking water was suspect and the air quality was a breath of cancer, he was incredibly optimistic. He was just waiting for this Janet thing, or something like it. Of course, it was one last trip "below board," as he put it. He'd gone off the meds a month before. Running and lifting weights had become his answer for everything. Even though he was drunk last night, he'd still jogged three miles, and had come home shouting about meth labs and dead animals in the abandoned lot.

When she followed him to Gary, when they'd given up on New York, she discovered this town was Rich. Park waters a beautiful polluted green and failed manufacturing. Liz gripped the wheel and leaned hard on the gas. She was greeted with fifty billboards on the highway—Had an accident? Suffering from *Black Lung, Cancer, Emphysema? Free Complete Pulmonary Evaluation. Don't give up. Plinski and Danforth can help! Night Angels. Gentlemen's Club. Whispers. Discount Furs. Impress her!* Yep. Fast money.

Rich still hadn't texted when Liz pulled into Victor's, the last strip club before the Illinois state line. It was a favorite not just with truckers, but with people not wanting to pay Chicago's strip club prices. It was a strange crowd. It had a few patrons who looked burned out and ready to hide.

She parked behind the building, hiding her car from the road. She lit a cigarette and struggled with her prescription bottle. She needed people with their shit together. She craved it. But she also wanted people who were real, and that was sort of the rub, why she moved someplace rural. Her mom's family and friends were fake. Brooklyn had been full of fakes. Now she was way the hell and gone from where she thought she would be. She tipped her head back, swallowed, put the envelope in her purse.

Inside, she scanned Victor's. Janet was nowhere. Liz sat down at the bar, ordered a whiskey and waited for the Xanax to kick in.

This was one of those dive places to strip. She had always done better, made a grand a night. Don't talk to her about daddy issues or hearts of gold. That was the mythology of stripping. And she had no problem going back if needed.

But dancing at this place would be like working at Denny's if you were a good waitress. Depressing. She downed her whiskey and ordered another. A dude who looked out of place, a guy with longish black hair was giving her the eye. He looked like Joaquin Phoenix.

Her phone buzzed. Rich. *Where the fuck are you?*

Victor's. Answer your texts next time! No response. She laid down a veiled fuck you. *Get a ride with Derek!*

Derek managed to be less reliable than Rich. If Rich was Gary, Derek was Gary's dirty cousin. His ass was supposed to be at Victor's, too. Of course, he was nowhere to be found. Liz had texted him, too. Surprise. No response.

Joaquin's double was giving her a gross look, but she was bored, so she didn't stop him from taking the seat beside her. "Hey, I'm Cary."

He smiled at her and continued. "You wouldn't believe it. They were shooting a movie down at the river. Some cop show," he said. He was drunk but still seemed a little dangerous.

"No, they weren't," said Liz. She shot her whiskey to make it more tolerable to talk to him.

"Is that hard to believe? I guess beautiful girls have a hard time believing secondhand stories."

"It's a little early to flirt like your life depended on it."

"Don't flatter yourself. Did you ever see *The Silence of the Lambs?*" said Cary.

"Everyone has seen *The Silence of the Lambs*." She stressed the word The. He didn't notice.

"You know how that guy just fools girls into getting into his van."

"That movie is so disturbing."

"But you know what I'm talking about?"

"I've seen the movie. It's on cable all the time, dipshit."

"Well, you know how he just gets them to climb in the back of the truck, and then like pushes that heavy piece of furniture into them. Then he gets them to his house. But after he kills them, he weights them in the river."

Liz hoped he wasn't the kind of drunk to spool out unconscious thoughts. "It wasn't my favorite movie." She slowly wiped her mouth and raised her hand for another drink.

"Doesn't have to be. I'm just saying, that down there by the river, they had kind of one of those dead-body-in-the-reeds-thing happening. And that's what they were filming."

"Really?" She tried to convey she wasn't interested. She stopped mid-sip, when the bartender gave her the "too-fast" eye. Everyone feels they need to parent an attractive woman. But they can fuck off.

"Yeah. It's hidden back on the Calumet. I guess they're going to make money in some poor town where they don't have to pay much to use the land. Movies are kind of a big business anymore what with all the franchises."

Liz turned to look at him like he wasn't for real.

"It's all the Marvel Comic adaptations," said Cary.

Something in this dude reminded her of her brother. He and her mom were huge film nerds. The three of them went to the Music Box weekly. She relaxed a little. "You seem like a freak for movies." And also an idiot, she thought.

"Me and my mom used to go a lot. When I lived in the city," said Cary.

They swapped a couple stories about Chicago. Liz had forgotten Janet and was drunk by the time Derek arrived and gave her a shitty look. "Bitch," he mouthed from the door. He walked up to Cary, picked up the dude's whiskey and downed it. "Fuck off," he said.

Cary laughed.

"Derek," said Liz. She put a hand over her drink and smiled up at him.

Derek said nothing, but nodded toward the back of the bar, where Janet sat alone in a booth, looking freaked out.

"You fucked up, Liz," said Derek.

Liz realized she had been talking to this dope, Cary, long enough to miss Janet's arrival. Fuck. Liz threw down a twenty. "Nice talking to you."

Rich was standing at the door. He had spotted her and looked super-pissed she was talking to some dude. Rich was sensitive, but everyone was, so Liz couldn't fault him. It was hard to tell when someone was really going to leave. Once, he did become jealous over a bartender hitting on her, and he called her nothing but "slut" for a month. She'd matched him with "pussy" for that same month, aware of the irony. To her, it wasn't a bad thing. Fuck him if he took it negatively. She wanted to explain the irony to him but didn't have the energy.

When they walked to the table, Liz tried to pry her mind out of the film talk—specifically *The 400 Blows*, which she had studied in film class. Cary was going on about it. Some dude in Indiana knew about French New Wave. Amazing. She couldn't get her head back on their task and Rich looked like an alien, sad and pathetic, just staring at her.

He took her arm. "I called you," he said. "Did you bring the moeny?"

Liz pulled her arm away. "Of course. Don't be stupid."

"I didn't see you guys. I thought you pussed out," said Janet. She smoked her cigarette incredibly fast, and she was so high the words spilled out in an explanation of what she'd done since they saw her.

"Let's go outside," said Derek.

"Wait a sec. Are we leaving?" said Liz.

"I ain't doing shit here," said Derek.

Rich's fingers pressed into her upper arm, and he smelled of cigarettes and booze. The thrash metal made it hard to hear, so she leaned closer. "Let's get this done," he said. It sounded meaningful, but he was looking at Derek.

There were those times in Liz's life when a realization began to surface but retreated again without warning, some small fish swimming to the top of her consciousness. Who knew what it meant? But she stood there and blinked.

"Hold on. I have to piss," she said. She wrenched her arm away, and Rich looked at the floor. "That's what I thought," she said. Whatever optimism he exuded last night was gone, and his expression had become one of terror.

Liz ran to the bathroom, feeling nauseated and breathing heavily. She reached into her purse, pulled out the envelope and fumbled with it. She stopped. She took a deep breath and wished she were already in Chicago. She could just walk out and tell Rich to fuck off, drive to see her mom, who would listen without judgment. She stared at her reflection in the mirror, her pale skin feathered with lines. She pulled two grand from her thick stack. She would give them the two grand, say she wouldn't have the rest until Monday. She'd say her mom still had it. It was safe.

Someone was knocking. "Fucking wait a second," she said. She reached into the paper-towel dispenser, slid the remaining eleven thousand as far up as she could get it. She scraped her hand on the lip of the dispenser trying to do it.

"Hurry the fuck up," a woman yelled through the door.

She thrust her hand under the sink tap. She could easily get this when she came back for her car. If something worse happened, some stripper would find it when washing the stink off. More power to that bitch. This place was an inglorious, industrialized strip-tank. Hopefully, she would realize she could do better.

She cleaned away the makeup smudges in the mirror and walked out.

Rich was waiting. "What the fuck? Are you trying to make me crazy?"

"Nothing," said Liz.

"Don't ruin this," said Rich.

After all that, Rich and Derek "had to talk to the owner" and made Liz and Janet wait outside not speaking, Janet slowly sipping her flask and staring at the highway. "You're an awful bitch," said Liz.

Janet took a drink from her flask and didn't turn around. Whatever camaraderie there was between the dudes inside, it was totally gone between Janet and Liz. Shivering, Liz watched the highway, too.

Derek and Rich came out. Rich told Janet. "We'll follow."

"Another location?" said Janet.

"I said we ain't talking here," said Rich.

They followed Janet's Chevy past Denny's, the Citgo, out of Gary, and south on the highway. Liz thought of Cary, her family, and school. She watched Rich drink bourbon from a Coke bottle, smoke a cigarette. Liz rubbed her arm absently where he'd grabbed her. The soreness was small, a bloom that promised to open larger.

When his depression would hit, Rich could be nearly immobilized. Last time he hit bottom, he didn't leave the apartment in Bushwick for days, and Liz was surprised he didn't off himself. But once he could crawl his way out of the mud, he came up swinging. She'd mistakenly thought he was brooding, only to find out he was mentally ill. Then the olanzapine.

Rich turned around, eyes narrow, a perfectly rigid face. He had explained this plan like she were a child as they ate Thai food at this dive near her crappy room rental. Janet had come by the stuff by screwing a dealer.

"You think it's stolen?" said Liz.

"I know it is. Now she's going to steal it from that jackass Tom."

"Not surprising."

"Nobody gives a shit about her," he said.

"Yeah."

"It's not like she's a good person, anyway. She's a cock-sucking thief," he said.

Calling Janet a cocksucker was, at best, obvious. Liz hated it when Rich said stupid things. But it also inspired pitty, which she couldn't resist. She sometimes felt that this compulsion to be helpful, to be agreeable when she wasn't feeling it, would be her downfall.

"It'll be easy. I promise," he said.

"As long as the money I'm fronting doesn't get lost in all this," said Liz. Liz didn't mind double-crossing Janet, either. She felt like everyone had a part to play, and Janet was playing the victim this time. It became clear they were going to make Janet the dog in this. Liz had been the dog before, so it was only fair she come out on top this time.

Derek was driving like a maniac past the wind farms. He grumbled that Janet was speeding up. "She's trying to get away," he said.

"Why the fuck would she do that?" said Rich.

"Because she doesn't have dick. She smoked it all," said Derek.

"I'll beat the shit out of her if that's the case."

"You're always talking big," said Liz. She lit a cigarette. "If she smoked it that fast, she'd be dead."

"Fuck you, Liz." Derek looked at Rich nervously, to see if he crossed a line. But Rich didn't care. Apparently, he wanted to be defended. He cleared his throat and threw his cigarette out the passenger window.

There were a couple weeks, when they all first met, when Liz had been intermittently sleeping with both of them. In Derek's more contemplative moods, he rambled about his days as a Marine. It nearly always degenerated into a rhetorical discussion of violence, in which Derek stared off in the distance. It felt stagey. Liz distrusted that he was ever sad about killing people. She doubted he really knew the difference between the real and the unreal. He was pissed when she ended it. But how could she deal with his profound ambivalence?

She took out her phone and checked her messages, texted a friend from Chicago, and slipped the phone into her coat, watching the towering poles, the airplane propellers spinning slowly, in lazy discontinuity. Rich gave her a half-smile with a crooked attempt at levity, reached back, and smacked her leg. It didn't feel right.

"C'mon. It's easy," he said.

"It's not," said Liz.

"She kind of deserves it." He raised an eyebrow and made a face.

"That may be true," said Liz. "We all kind of deserve shitty things."

Last fall she'd had a particularly rough time with Rich. It was partly her fault. She had her head in the clouds, constantly oscillating between thinking too largely and letting herself drop back to reality, knowing all the while you had to work with your own assets. She stopped stripping for a while. She cried a lot.

He was always having those crazy stars in his eyes. Rich could fool people, because he could be fooled himself. He was always lured by money. And he wanted all of it. He could be greedy. Last time he thought he had a fast deal turning over those cars with Derek, he'd really gotten in shape. Talked only of money. He kept his body perfect, ran each morning and came home in his sweats, flushed. He looked good. He'd cook deer meat in the slow cooker—his mom's recipe. Predictably, he talked about his parents, then. It was at that moment she couldn't stand him. She felt mismatched, like his bullshit was hers. She did want to protect them both. With the seventy-five thousand they were going to get an apartment in Roger's Park, better jobs, a better shrink. Liz would go back to school, and if they parted ways, they'd both be better off. She hadn't told him yet.

On a dirt road, they paralleled the river, past poplars and oaks heavy with snow, and half-shattered sheets of river ice, where the water sometimes bubbled through the fissures like oil. They were headed into the woods. No one driving by would notice them, but you could still catch sight of the highway over the rise. There was one burned-out building but nothing else. Shit. It was poor here. But beautiful. New York had its interesting neighborhoods, museums, but let's face it, she spent most of her time in her hovel in Bushwick. New York was for the rich.

The low-hanging branches spanned the road, as if heavy with child, and reached backward toward the rushing water. But it was deserted, and she thought about Victor's and the Low Down and Ms. Turley, and the trashiest of towns. If you wanted decline, but beauty, this was the film location.

They pulled into a deserted campsite, near a pit of charred wood, and parked. They got out of Derek's car, and he walked around to the trunk, where he pulled out some Budweisers and set the six-pack on a log. "Here they are," he said, as if the beer had been missing.

Liz watched the Calumet rush by, destined for its putrescent state by the lake. People still fished and swam in Lake Michigan where the Calumet rushed in, filled with industrial runoff and pollution. She marveled at the swift current, free of large debris, brownish gray, fast and deep.

Derek and Rich exchanged looks and were shot-gunning their beers, too busy drinking to speak. Rich was entering one of those detached states where it looked like he didn't even know her, like he could see right through to the back of her skull. It chilled the fuck out of her.

Liz began to worry about everything now. "What if Janet doesn't have it on her?"

"She's got it," said Derek. "I seen it in her purse."

"Does she have both bags?" said Liz. "Because we need all three pounds."

"She does." Derek looked at Rich.

Janet got out of the car. "You got my fucking money?" she said. "I'm done dicking around with this." She came toward them.

Liz opened her mouth to tell Janet it was a consignment deal; that was Liz's role—the mouthpiece. She was going to tell her there was only two grand—down from fifteen—sorry about your fucking luck. Then when the argument started, she'd tell them all where to go. The guys had promised no rough stuff. But Janet and her drugs would still part ways. Sometimes Liz hated herself. In those few seconds, Liz sensed she would come out with scars, collateral damage for involving herself with the wrong people, the wrong shit.

"Janet, this is how it's going to go down." Liz's voice grew large.

"Don't you fucking talk to me. I'm dealing with them."

Liz was ready to put Janet in her place. But a car turned off the highway and distracted her. Across the field, past an expanse of white, there was a growing bloom of whipping snow as an old Chevy sped down the dirt road. They were so far in the middle of nothing. Undercover cop, thought Liz.

"Who the fuck is that?" said Janet.

The car gathered speed, spraying up snow and mud. The driver seemed too drunk to be the police. Liz's neck prickled, a snaking up, like cold water thrown over her bare back. She kept thinking fuck. Fuck. Fuck. Like it was the only word left in her mind. And she began regretting everything, even being alive.

She wondered if maybe it was what some people in this Bible Belt town called the Holy Spirit. But then she didn't believe in that shit, and she hated herself for being reductive. She was feeling freaked out, and that's all. The car slammed to a stop.

Somehow she was not entirely surprised to see Cary. Something hadn't felt right about it. He was too smug. She also hadn't realized he was seven feet. He wore steel toed boots, had a gun visible beneath his open jacket.

"Hello, you pussies."

As she again considered Cary's unbelievable height, he pulled a gun out and so did Derek—something from the military, a high-grade weapon, probably illegal. They pointed them at Janet. Only Rich looked rabbity, frightened, like he might fly apart, causing Liz to silently will him to look at her. When Derek yelled something unintelligible, Rich pulled out a gun as well.

Someone shot Janet, who fell over lightly, like she'd just lost her balance, like she'd been walking along and slipped on the ice. She put her hands up to her cheek, smearing mud over her face, blood shooting from her ear and neck. It didn't last, she settled down softly, eyes open.

"Holy shit," said Liz. "Holy shit." She was the only one without a gun. But only one shot killed Janet. And it was from the psycho she'd met at the bar. Jesus, she should trust her instincts. She stood still, feeling like an idiot.

Rich looked freaked. "Oh baby. Oh baby," he said. He actually hopped around.

"C'mon. Do it," said Cary.

"Christ almighty. Fuckity-fuck," said Rich.

"Calm the fuck down," said Cary. "There's no splitting. And you pussies can't do the shit work."

Liz stood still in the cold, unable to stop considering how stupid Rich was for saying fuckity-fuck. She didn't want this to be her last thought. But she couldn't help herself. Fuckity-fuck. Fuckity-fuck. He even stuttered.

"We have somewhere to be," said Cary. "And it's going to suck to bury these bodies in the dark. Ground's frozen enough."

"Wait," said Rich. Had he somehow had a change of heart? Even Liz knew they would shoot her no matter what.

Cary raised the Glock, shot her in the leg. She could hear screams, but they were Rich's, as if he had been shot.

"Nope. Done deal," said Cary. "Like so many other

things, lost in the river."

Again, Liz regretted that this blowhard's words would be the last she heard, as she lay in the snow, on fire and fighting the slip of passing out.

"You fucking crazy asshole," said Rich.

"Too late," said Cary.

Derek stood above her not looking like himself. He aimed at her chest, as if he couldn't stand to mar her face. How stupid. It would feel like a force, a hard weight crushing her. Her death wasn't even her own, like a movie, however clichéd that thought was, just another woman not reading the signs properly, no better or worse than anyone else. She came to the realization, she'd been bored for months, and now she wasn't. She began to regret.

Rich was shivering, holding his gun loosely as he slowly drew his skinny arms over his chest. He stared straight at her. He grew dimmer as she imagined some bitch getting the money before he did, his optimism finally meeting an end. Thank god. They'd never bury her body in this frozen ground, either. Both women would be found in the river, by the police force, its members more numerous than the fish. That seemed fine, preferable, even. Goodbye to Gary. But she felt bad for her mom. She was finding peace floating away from the pollution, except for the lunacy of Rich's warped, high-pitched voice, screaming like an idiot.

FOURTEENER

The detective had called six times, twice while he was in the Uber. His friends said this cop was an asshole. But they weren't used to being treated with suspicion. They had that suburban sensibility—naive and coddled—like him.

Really, except for Jake, everyone had a childhood of soccer leagues and malls—a sleepy existence punctuated with weekend ski trips. Six-foot-two and fit, Björn could have walked out of an ad for an Aspen lodge before he'd moved to LA and started working for a living. Life had been easy until his parents pseudo-adopted Jake.

Björn's anxiety churned with the jostling of TSA checks, line-pacing dogs, and the incessant chatter of his seatmate. The moment he saw his parents waiting at baggage, he longed for his one-hitter. They hugged a little too hard, told him he had to talk to the officer. His father said, "He's been to the house."

"You're not in any trouble." His mom's face was pale. "Just tell them what you saw." She shrugged but wouldn't look him in the eyes.

Björn called Iverson and agreed to visit the Denver Police Department.

They put him in a tiny room with a patched vinyl

couch and a camera. Everyone was ridiculously nice, but he was cold, his legs wet from the sideways snow that soaked his jeans. He waited an hour and grew weary of the camera. When Iverson came in, Björn was shocked to see they were the same age. He had a full beard, dark-rimmed glasses, a flannel shirt, and tight corduroy pants—the outfit of a punk bass player, not someone in law enforcement. They could have been twins.

"Born, I just want to hear what you think happened in Estes Park."

"Björn. It's Scandinavian."

"Yeah. Whatever. Scandinavian," he said.

His friends weren't kidding about the combativeness. Björn smiled, making a show of cooperation. Yet thinking of that day brought the image-—Jake tumbling from the rocky outcrop, his body disturbing the pines, then sliding over scree as he struggled to grab a boulder.

Björn's friends hadn't seen Jake's fall, but their trash-talk insinuated it wasn't an accident. Björn wanted to be honest, but his version also sounded incriminating. This cop might be fair, but Björn couldn't be sure. Since the minutes before Jake fell were a big blank nothing, he didn't have reliable insight, either. He felt inept.

Björn shrugged. "I have no idea how it happened," he said. The room grew smaller, Iverson stared, and the feeling of being in trouble was jarring. Björn began to overshare, about Jake being a seasoned hiker, a skilled climber, too self-possessed to consider suicide.

"He joined a club to climb all fifty-three of the four-teeners," said Björn. "He'd knocked off ten from the list even before we went to Crested Butte."

Björn didn't say "bag" though that's the language of

bravado Jake would have used. To mimic the swagger would have been to embody Jake for a moment. He couldn't do it.

"What's a fourteener?"

"Fourteen thousand feet high. I thought you were from Colorado."

"Nebraska. Originally."

Björn rolled his eyes. "Well. It's a thing here. As far as I know, until Jake, no one has fallen from the Glacier Gorge Trail. It's a day hike. My parents do it." Björn suddenly worried about Hailey.

"How would you describe Ms. Myers' behavior?"

There it was. "Hailey was upset. Really upset," said Björn.

"Was she sensitive to what everyone else was going through?"

"She was freaked. We all were," said Björn.

"So you didn't like the way she handled it?"

"She handled it fine." A lie. Hailey had handled it with bizarre and insensitive ranting. She threw a glass at Björn's head. She told everyone to fuck off and walked out of the hotel without another word.

After the interview, Björn stopped at a dispensary, but he could barely keep it together on the drive to his parents. Why had he lied? When people lied on *Dateline*, it seemed so obvious. Did he just compare his friend's death to *Dateline*? God, he was turning into a piece of shit.

Björn ignored his parents' questions and went to his old room. He slept until one o'clock the next day, getting up only to Christmas shop with his dad. Denver was negative four, overcast, the sidewalks of their neighborhood coated in gray snow. Björn instantly missed the desert climate, confirming his suspicion that he no longer felt at home anywhere.

Christmas Eve, his family watched the evening news on local channel KMGH. Jake's mother talked to local anchor Jane Gibbon, and gave an emotional plea with the statement, "Justice for Jake." Jake hadn't seen his mother in ten years. She'd struggled with addiction, and it seemed she had emerged from nowhere, hammering any law enforcement agent who would listen—the local police, the state troopers, the FBI.

Hailey called Björn and asked him to visit Snowmass. She was now a suspect. Hailey's wealthier-than-shit dad was a hedge fund manager—second house, private jet, indoor pool, home theater, workout facility, everything. Mr. Meyers had a preternatural degree of protectiveness over his only daughter, yet here she was waiting.

Inside a steamed atrium, Hailey reclined in a patio chair. A lone yellow raft floated in the turquoise pool beside her. She was baked, eyes glazed and unfocused. She'd bundled in a flannel, hoodie, and leggings, a perfunctory look given her penchant for diamonds and handmade jewelry from the Highlands.

Björn sat down. He lit the glass pipe.

With an even tone, Hailey talked of nothing—her yoga class, her sister, her mom's trip to Turkey. She periodically checked her phone. She was looking at Facebook. Björn wanted to ask about the cops, about Iverson. Hailey refused eye contact. Suddenly, she set down the pipe. "I'm hungry," she said.

They picked up two orders of veal tenderloin from a four-star restaurant in the village and parked in a turnout near Capitol Peak. Hailey spread a napkin and took small bites of veal and stared at the fading ridgeline. It was dusk, so there wasn't much to see. Finally, she said, "We should probably go back since it's dark." She closed her take-out box and started the Humvee.

"Jesus, Hailey, tell me about the police," said Björn.

"Oh." She acted as if she hadn't thought of it. "My dad's so freaked he's retained three lawyers."

"Already?" But of course he had.

Björn was sometimes ashamed of the awe he felt over her family's money. This Humvee had been her eighteenth birthday present. A monster, it spanned both lanes of the narrow road. That birthday, her parents also rented a cabin for twenty friends so they could ski the backcountry. Mr. Myers and his girlfriend stayed in a separate condo up the road. Björn had made out with Hailey during seven minutes in heaven. Jake was there and might have made out with her, too. It was very inauspicious but innocent, groping someone next to a kegerator. Somehow, she was still that same girl. He knew he wasn't going to be able to make her feel better. Not really.

"I might have to go to fucking prison. Do you know what that's like?" she said.

"Of course." They'd never had a friend get arrested, not even for something small, like underage drinking or petty vandalism.

"Don't be glib," said Hailey. She navigated the behemoth over the mountain highway. A car approaching from a switchback had to pull over. Hailey didn't even slow to pass.

"You haven't been arrested," said Björn.

"I just don't fucking think I can take prison. I'd

kill myself."

"Jesus, Hailey."

Only part of this was melodrama. Hailey always pushed the usual social limits. In high school, she constantly stole Maker's Mark from her job at Whole Foods, even though the manager threatened to call her parents. She climbed to the school's roof on a dare. In protest of school policies about leggings, she wore pajamas to class. Somehow, she didn't seem unstable then. Her friends, including Björn and Jake, wanted her to push boundaries and didn't care if she got in trouble. They lived through her.

Björn took a deep breath. "I didn't tell them about the keys," he said. They turned down her narrow drive, and Hailey skirted the thick snow-banks.

"What about them?" she said, like it was the first she'd heard of the most damning evidence.

"C'mon. At some point I'm going to have to tell them. I wanted to tell you first," he said.

"You mean something about Jake planning to return my apartment keys? Allison told me that. There's nothing I'm ashamed of," said Hailey.

Björn willed himself to make her feel better, but he couldn't pull up any genuine emotion. She parked next to his car. "Forgive me," she said.

When he looked over, she was shaking. Björn freaked for a second but realized she could mean multiple things. He let the comment lay between them until she said she had to go to bed.

☾

Björn was sick of his parents' questions. Even after they were exhausted from the ritual of cocktails, presents, and frying lefse, they still asked if Jake may have been depressed. Björn said he didn't know. But it brought to mind every testy comment, every instance Jake seemed out of sorts.

The day of the funeral, Björn's parents questioned Jake's father, Kent. Kent sat away from everyone, on a divan with Jake's mother, her mouth a hard line, refusing conversation with anyone. "Goddamn," she kept saying. "Goddamn." Kent held a framed picture of Jake in one hand as he spoke. "He was so upbeat. I didn't think he could get depressed," he said.

More photos were scattered across the casket——at the center, a photo from a climb up Pike's Peak. Tan and windblown, Jake smiled, his arm disappearing outside the frame. Someone had cropped Hailey.

When police questioned everyone about Hailey's character, it was all high-school shit-talk—"You know Hailey—she throws money around ... is melodramatic ... is difficult, etc." But this time, they had a very real audience.

Allison Beaks, Hailey's former best friend, who'd been with them on the trail, defended herself with the statement, "I just want some answers," as if those answers were tangible, fixed items scattered like seeds across the ravine. Of course, it got Allison on the news, and she did look good, after all.

Björn wondered why their friends didn't remember Jake as he was—imperfect and difficult. At times, Jake could be an asshole.

Senior year, during their free period, Jake often

slumped in a library chair with his hood up and slept, which was against the rules. Exceptionally tall, he was hard to miss. Faculty hated him, but the teacher stationed at the information desk, Ms. Banks, probably hated him most. That day Jake sat carving his name into the table.

Banks leaned over the circular desk and loudly whispered, "Jake!" Beside her was straight-A student Jill Adams, in leggings and North Face, who had complained Jake verbally harassed her in the stacks by saying a word over and over again until it "made her ill."

"I'm about to get busted," said Jake. He watched Jill Adams jab a finger his direction.

"For what?" whispered Björn.

"For saying a word to Jill Adams like fifty times."

"What was the word?" whispered Björn.

"Clit."

Jake could be weird and immature, and sometimes kind of mean. He didn't even see it coming, that Jill would go to Banks. "Jake Matthews, come up here now."

Jake turned around. He could have gotten up and apologized. But he did something stupid. He made a gun with his thumb and forefinger, just a real simple gesture, like a gangster with a revolver, and shot. One year after Columbine in Colorado, you just couldn't do that. There were shooter drills for months, metal detectors at the doors, sirens in the hallways.

During his two-week suspension, Jake let his social life die. Often, he was in and out of foster care, sometimes going back to live with Kent, the only parent able to pull it together enough for temporary guardianship. Both parents had serious addiction issues, not just meth, which was enough, but they were hoarders. His first visit, Jake explained, while staring at the ground, that sometimes those things go hand-in-hand. But in the middle of his suspension, Kent sent his son back to foster care.

Disgusted by his living conditions, Björn's parents helped Jake with practical things: his driver's ed classes, his license, a bank account funded monthly with five hundred dollars through high school. In the winter, they took him to the slopes, paid for his skis and lift passes. Björn and Jake skied together down black runs in Vail and Breckenridge. Sometimes Jake still acted indebted to Björn, as if they were unequal friends. It made Björn feel shitty. But mentioning this to his parents was off limits.

Jake's foster parents lived in a failed housing development, down one of those streets ending in nothing. It was in that nothingness that Jake liked to shoot clay pigeons, bottles, and cans with his foster father.

Björn called Jake during the suspension. Did he want to do some rock-wall climbing at his parents' club? Normally they'd hang out with their group—Allison, Greg, Tim. But he figured Jake might feel antisocial. He'd give him time to bullshit.

"Not feeling the athletic club, man," said Jake. "Let's shoot pigeons."

So Björn sat in a camp chair and watched Jake blow things apart. Annoying. "You're having a shit year," said Björn.

"If only I had the nerve to show them what I think," said Jake. He loaded his foster dad's semi-auto Ithaca and shot.

"God. That sounds fucking scary."

"They've been shitty," said Jake.

"They have," said Björn. He didn't say more. Lately, there was always something wrong with Jake. He suspected they were both thinking about Hailey. Both were friends with her, but neither had asked her out. He thought about admitting his attraction to her.

But Jake held up the gun. "I wish I had your parents."

Jesus. Jake wasn't even thinking of Hailey. Björn felt guilty that he'd been so lucky with his parents. He resented the guilt.

That year after high school, the relationship with Hailey had been good for Jake. But by sophomore year of college, it was hard to tell which of them was more toxic. On Björn's phone, there was a photo of Hailey in Utah. Her hair was windswept from the desert breeze. She stood on a cliff, an arm around Jake. She appeared nervous, staring at some fixed point outside the frame. Björn couldn't look at this picture without feeling overwhelmed with love and misery.

It was late May and her dad had funded a trip for the three of them—Jake, Hailey, and Björn. Hailey paid for their lodging in Bryce Canyon National Park, Escalante, and Canyonlands. For a month, they hiked slot canyons, stood on plateaus, and marveled at towering sandstone cliffs. They talked about their difficulties securing jobs, as the desert got unbearably cold against a ribbon of pink sky. They went back to five-star hotels, ordered room service, got high. In the morning, from their heated pools, they watched the sun rise.

One night, Björn came back to the room and heard them shouting. They had locked him out of the suite. He heard Hailey saying, "How can you live this way?" and Jake kept saying she didn't understand "shit about his life." Then there was crying. Björn listened far too long. It was unconscionable to stand and stare at the door.

He went down to the bar and charged shots of Lagavulin to Hailey's room account. She came down red-faced and glassy-eyed. She'd paid for a separate room for him. He got really pissed, but took the room, and swam in the lap pool alone. He ached for her and swam laps, becoming too exhausted to care.

The week Jake died, their friends joined them in a hike over the Maroon Bells circuit-—dangerous saddles, dry meadows cracked by heat, fields of avalanche deposits. It was the end of a sixth-month stint of climbing and hiking to avoid the disappointment of looking for jobs. Of course, Hailey continued to pay. She rented three suites in the Oasis, a desert spa for the hyper-elite— politicians, celebrities, multinational CEOs.

The Oasis had the usual impressive private pool, sauna, and heated floors. It didn't surprise Björn, with its modern angles and endless glass and wood. But everyone talked about changing hotels.

"The more nervous Hailey gets," said Jake at the bar with Björn and Greg, "the more she taps into her Dad's Amex."

"This is more than we need," said Greg. "That's all I'm saying."

"No shit." Jake hadn't had a job in a year, and he snapped every time they discussed money for gas or food.

It became a thing. He and Hailey fought everywhere. Jake disintegrated behind a series of repetitive and tiresome complaints. It was all anyone could talk about. Of the six questioned, five friends made negative statements about Hailey and said she used her family's money to leverage friendships, that she was "emotionally selfish." Much of the animosity had a subtext of overall income disparity and class gap. But Björn never once felt Hailey's money was a bribe. Their aggression seemed petty and confusing.

It was on that trip he decided to tell Hailey how he felt, that she could do better than Jake. One night he waited outside their door listening to the muffled sounds of bodies and breath. He walked away feeling a disgust which shook him.

They should have gone home, but instead they all drove to a place outside Rocky Mountain National Park called Castle Cabins.

On the way, Jake stared out the window and complained. They were far enough out to see signs of fracking off the highway. At a gas station, a few hundred yards away, a guy in a hazmat suit sprayed a rusty substance toward a drainage ditch. He appeared otherworldly.

Jake snapped. "This is what's wrong. This is what's wrong." He pointed to the hazmat guy.

Sometimes, Jake had minutes of lucidity where he expounded on fracking, class gaps, credit crunches. His favorite thing to say was "those fuckers," whoever "those fuckers" were, anyone in authority, anyone with money.

It's not that Jake wasn't right. He could just be an unbearable asshole.

At Castle Cabins they all got drunk and high. For a few hours of reprieve, they played horseshoes and swam in the leafy pool. They all sat in front of the fire talking like nothing had ever gone wrong, that two of them hadn't been hurling really awful insults just days before. There weren't enough rooms, but no one cared. They passed out on the floor wherever they had stopped drinking.

In the middle of the night, Björn awoke to see Jake using his headlamp to look through his pack.

"What are you doing, man?" Björn wanted to remind Jake that he'd lost his mind if he was going to start out at 3:30 a.m. with the bears.

"Leave me alone," said Jake. He stopped searching his pack and let his shoulders fall. "I couldn't sleep anymore." He pulled out a set of keys and slipped them in his pocket.

"Hailey?"

"Shut up, man," whispered Jake. He looked back at Hailey's sleeping figure and motioned him outside.

They sat on the motel's front steps. They stared at the parking lot and the woods the roofline of distant cabins illuminated in the dusk. "Everything just seems so bad," said Jake. "I've had about enough."

"You going to move on?"

"I don't know. I just have to make some changes."

They left it at that. Björn brought his one-hitter and passed it to Jake.

"Listen, dude. I can't thank you and your parents enough for helping me out in high school."

He said this like it hadn't come up before. "That was five years ago. It's fine," said Björn.

"No. They're really different than other people, you know. Better."

Björn felt a repulsion that took a moment to shake it. His parents' generosity meant so much to Jake, and to Björn it meant nothing. His own self-absorption surprised him.

This was their last conversation. He had wanted to tell Jake—*you are more than this*. In the morning, they were hiking and Jake fell. Like a coward, Björn left his friends to handle the hospital, the cops, Jake's dad. He should have been able to hug Hailey, something, but he felt like screaming. He kept thinking about Jake as a ragdoll, sliding down the mountain. He drove back to Denver with his phone off.

Björn's parents finally found the courage to say what they'd resisted in August. They believed Jake was murdered, and it crushed them. It had taken a few martinis for it to come out. At five am he found his mom on the couch downstairs, crying like she had when his grandmother showed signs of dementia and needed a new care facility.

"He was our family," she said. "Doesn't it kind of drive you crazy?"

"Of course," said Björn. But he was more convinced that Jake had jumped. His fatigue and ambivalence made him go back and forth, a prolonged torture. Everything became a what if. What if they'd had a real talk? What if they'd stopped hiking after Maroon Bells?

Björn promised to call. He waited on hold for thirty minutes, and when Iverson answered, he rushed through his explanation. Jake intended to return Hailey's keys. Jake wanted to "clean up" and "put stuff behind him."

Iverson didn't seem to give a shit. "I already know that," he said. "Born, do you know anything about Jake's criminal record?"

"Björn. And Jake didn't have a criminal record."

"As a matter of fact, he did. Broke into his stepfather's house. Stole a rifle."

"What? No," said Björn. "His stepfather was like totally open with him."

"You didn't notice Jake acting depressed before he jumped?"

"No."

"How close were you?"

"Very." God what an ass. "Are you charging Hailey?"

"Björn, you have anything else to tell me?"

"Uh. I guess that was it," said Björn. He felt childish, as if he'd wasted Iverson's time.

But Iverson judged Jake from one action. He only knew Jake through the distorted lens of his death. It wasn't fair to reduce him to a three-second event. He returned to the memory: Jake, a ragdoll, his head hitting a tree, his body sliding through brush, his side crashing against a boulder.

Squeezing the phone, Björn blurted, "Fuck you." He waited for blowback, but Iverson had hung up.

When Björn told his parents the detective ruled it a suicide, his mother sat down at the kitchen table, and covered her face with her hands. They couldn't believe it. Maybe Iverson was ignoring Hailey's involvement because she was rich. "Surely they're not going to drop it. Jake just wasn't the type to do something like that." She sobbed and Björn felt his empathy ebbing away.

Why couldn't his parents see Jake was flawed? Wasn't it less real to blindly love someone without recognizing their faults? At least he understood Jake. Somehow, his parents had become such hypocrites. They wanted someone to blame.

A month after Jake's death, Hailey flew to LA. He made dinner and they tried binge-watching *The X-Files* but ended up turning it off to talk about Jake. "His family abused him in all ways," she said, stressing the all. "He always had that gun in his truck."

Björn felt momentarily disgusted. "That just makes me feel like shit."

"Sorry." She shifted to complaining about their friends. No one called or texted. She said they were assholes. She said everyone was an asshole. She downed her drink. They finished half a pint of Jim Beam, sinking into the shapeless pillows of Björn's shitty futon, until her foot gently rested on his thigh.

He never asked if she pushed Jake. Of course, she'd told the police he jumped. But now she said they'd been having one of their drag-out fights. He'd grabbed her shoulder to stop her from running up a trail cut so narrowly into the mountain. Intellectually, Björn knew it was an accident, that she had helplessly watched him lose footing, an easy thing to do with so much exposure. She said it was her fault. In his heart, Björn agreed. Yet he sympathized.

Making out seemed easy. He pressed his knee between her thighs. It was hard to tell if she thought they were wrong. She hid her face in his shoulder the whole time, making him feel like a stand-in for someone else. He wanted to stop, salvage his pride, but couldn't. For so long, he'd needed Hailey to think he was decent.

When Björn got up for water, his head was gummy. He floated to the kitchen, came back to see her head bowed. She had a hand on either knee, and sat stiff and unmoving on the couch, clearly angry with herself. They both were congenial the next day, but she flew home early instead of driving north to hike in Sequoia National Park.

He sat on the concrete pad behind his apartment and thought about how wrong he was. He even coiled in the chair like she had done, hands to knees as if he could mimic her emotional state. They were similar, and the prior night just seemed an extension in a long history of the three of them. Maybe she didn't think so.

After college, Björn thought that if he drove from Denver to Los Angeles it would transform him. He imagined a trip through the desert would help him see the Rockies in a new way. The Sierra Nevadas would offer a different perspective. He thought this so often, he convinced himself it was true. By the time he got back to California, his disgust and pity was something solid in his bones. "Jake cared more about everything than us shitheads," he told Hailey. A thousand times more. He thought Jake was better than either of them. He wondered if Hailey felt as guilty as he did. Probably. Yes. He was sure she did.

FAKER

Zoe stretched across the back seat and pressed her feet into my thigh, hair plastered to the fogged window. The only light was a flood lamp installed over the charred rendering plant to keep taggers away. She ripped open the Ziploc of weed. "Throw it," she said. She balanced the pipe on her bare stomach.

I tossed my Zippo, knowing she wouldn't break up now. The sweet smoke distracted from the work clothes I'd piled on the floor mat, but the truck still harbored the stench of ethanol and birds.

She passed the bowl and scrolled through her phone before settling on Robyn.

"You aren't mad?" I said.

"Not at you."

I could feel the girl I cheated with, Amy Blake, in the truck, imagined her crouched behind the head-rest, haunting us with a judgmental stare. I wasn't over her. She was brainy, belonged to clubs like Latin and Physics. Blond, she wore tiny fishbone braids tight at her temples, had a tattoo of an osprey with blood-tipped wings. Her fraternal twin served a sentence in juvie for something small, selling pot. She said, "It's hard when your best friend is missing." Lately, I'd been thinking how important it was to get close to someone.

Still, Amy shouldn't have tried to get close to a cheater. I had spilled her secrets to Zoe and felt like shit about it. I lit the bowl.

"We're frenemies now," said Zoe.

Zoe had smashed my Pathfinder window with a yard-paver after she got the Snapchatted dick-pic from Amy. I had it coming. Friends at school said Zoe was abusive. But I'd recently had an epiphany, while debeaking chickens, clipping them cold because Dad wouldn't pay for electric cauterizing. While I was forced to sit on that stool, Dad cursed his debts and low subsidies. I listened to his speeches about being fair, being "rock-solid" loyal. When they deserve it, I thought, and began to set down the hens without clipping them.

Zoe put her foot on my chest and gently pushed, forcing my head against the glass. "You ruined my whole senior year, buddy." She reached over for the Gatorade, because the Pathfinder was now sauna hot. "And so did that cherub-faced bitch. You make me lose faith in the whole human race. I'm not exaggerating."

No. She never exaggerated. Zoe felt if people bothered to argue, it always graduated to physical consequences. For Zoe, words bloated when they hit daylight or Twitter. She was sensitive to being called rich. "People say it when they mean loser," she said. She threatened to kill herself when someone wrote CLUELESS on her locker. Most of my friends were on the disintegrating end of middle class and moved in tight groups. The mass of so many strained faces was more intense than *Brick* or *Elephant* or *Heathers*.

"We can still have a good time senior year," I said.

"Maybe. You'd have to make it right."

"Amy's not out to get you. It was just a stupid mistake," I said.

"Just know. If someone's against me, like she is, I wish the worst on them," said Zoe. "I think of their deepest fear and wish it so hard my head aches. Like when Coach Janice outed me about being in therapy, I wished a miscarriage on her."

"Jesus Christ. Not everyone is out to get you. Sometimes they're just doing their job. You don't have to think that dark shit. It's not good for you." It disgusted me and started that push and pull in my brain, the stuff of insomnia.

"It's just wishes." Zoe looked surprised. "It's private."

"Zoe," I said. "Some people deserve judgment and some don't. You have to come up with a personal code. Be judicious, for fuck's sake." It felt wise to give her advice, but also pompous.

Zoe snuggled into me, and I thought it would be OK. She swung her arm around and punched my chest. I could feel a pinecone-sized bruise blooming on my sternum.

When I was a kid, I stuck Highglo solar system decals to the ceiling and a *Star Wars* poster on the office wall. It hadn't been Dad's farm for years, but no one got rid of them, even though the stars were dingy and missing points.

Dad didn't notice my growing disgust with poultry farming, so he didn't complain when I hid in the trailer while they electrocuted "spent" hens. I answered the phone for auditors and fielded unscheduled animal welfare checks. I'd learned Quickbooks to avoid the battery cages. Dad thought it meant I would go into business with him. When it came up, he grinned in a way that made me uncomfortable.

My earbuds in, I thought of Amy, her busted-up family, and her absent brother, how they even laughed the same. I thought of how we killed all the male chicks, stuffing them in trash bags on day one. She said her brother shared the same moles, which didn't make genetic sense. Her belief they could entirely match freaked me.

Maybe Amy slept with guys to numb out over Kurt's absence. I couldn't fault her. But why couldn't I get over her? I had this recurring, intrusive image of her naked across her bed, in her parents' empty trailer, still wearing her Toms. A truck rumbled past with crates of birds, and I wanted to crawl from my skin, beat the shit out of the driver.

Dad walked in the office carrying a Miller High Life. Lately, he practically lived at the Showtime Lounge. He'd been wearing the same green flannel, and it was stained with coffee and something yellow. I'd worried he was sick, but he self-diagnosed: seasonal affective disorder. It didn't mean he was going to do anything about it.

"You're going to have to help me move my stuff out this weekend," said Dad. "Your mom and I are getting divorced." Just like that, he sipped his Miller.

I zoned out as he talked, his voice mingled with the buzzing of a maintenance guy weed-whacking. He was moving to Harkins Inn in Chauncey, just off the highway. He didn't have a lot, but he couldn't do it himself. The whites of Dad's eyes were polluted with broken blood vessels, and his deep voice cracked when he said Mom's name. He began using it formally at that moment. "Maureen." Dad took a long gulp of beer. I realized I wasn't surprised.

"Get your friend Tony to help, too," Dad said.

"Tony's not my friend."

"Just get him. Don't give me a hard time."

Tony lived ten minutes from our house and could easily come by. But I wasn't going to tell Tony Sayers my parents were fucking divorcing. Tony was a loser. I only called him for weed. He didn't even go to Wallerton because he'd been expelled for punching Zoe in the darkroom when she wouldn't give him head. That's how Zoe and I met in Photography 1.

When I asked why, Tony said he liked to show people "how dangerous it was to be weak." What did Tony know about people's weaknesses? He barely left the house, played Xbox all day. Believing Tony knew something about life was like pretending an avatar had feelings.

The day Tony was expelled, I knew I would end up at his house. I waited at the door and tackled him when he answered. He fell back and hit his head on the cheap wooden arm of his parents' old couch. He got a concussion.

Surprisingly, Mom had been proud, calling me a knight to Tony's parents. "He defends people. It's what he does," she said. "Blindly sometimes."

To me, she'd sincerely called me Batman. To my face. No irony or anything. I wasn't a kid in pajamas watching *Batman Beyond*, wishing I could be powerful. So manipulative. They'd both been on my nerves for a while. Maybe being apart would force them to embrace reality.

Tony helped me move Dad in exchange for twenty bucks. I wanted to tell him about Zoe and Amy but didn't. Dude would think I was bragging. Maybe I would be if I said it aloud.

Tony made fun of Dad for looking like Skeletor, because Dad was haggard that day, and he cried carrying the U-Haul boxes. At the end of the night, Dad was so upset he just threw me his own truck keys, told me to drive it home. He'd use the work truck for as long as he could. I sat in the driver's seat, outside Harkins Inn, and paid Tony. I punched the steering wheel and the truck let out a sharp bleat.

Tony lit a joint. "You seem pretty fucked-up, dude."

"I am," I said. "But I'd feel better if you'd help me with something."

"What?"

Dad had forgotten a box of records in his truck— old Fogerty, and Steely Dan, music Dad listened to while woodworking. I said, "Let's soak them in drain cleaner. Return them to their sleeves. Act like we don't know what happened." I didn't even know if that would do anything.

Tony laughed. "Mind fuck. Right on," he said. He buckled his seat belt. "Your dad needs to leave that shit behind anyway. That's probably stuff he listened to with your mom."

"Probably," I said. I squeezed the steering wheel until it was painful.

Feeling guilty, I sat in my parents' mudroom, still wearing my muck boots speckled with white shit and swirled with down. I smoked a joint right there and scrolled with one thumb through the naked pictures Zoe sent, but every so often I thought of Amy.

On the way to school, I was close to telling Zoe about Dad. She was manic, popping ProCentra from a blister pack and downing it with Dr. Pepper.

"I'm upset." She snaked her arms around her messenger bag. "My mom and dad backed out on getting me a car. And we haven't solved the Amy issue. I seriously think you hate me."

"I don't hate you, baby. I love you," I said.

"See, I know that. I just get crazy when that bitch texts me nonstop asking why we can't fix things. Because you fucked my boyfriend. And you're going to get it!" she shouted.

"She's a bitch," I said. I didn't mean it. As punishment, I bit my lip, tasted blood.

Zoe looked at me like I was nuts. "Are you kidding? You don't mean that," she said. "And don't pull around by the gym, I don't want to walk that far. I have these fucktard shoes on," she said. I stopped at the cafeteria.

"You know I'm just going to lose it one of these days," she said. "It would be nice if my boyfriend could actually make up for things." She slammed the door.

I felt hammered by the time I walked to homeroom, like raw meat. But then what did meat feel like, cooked or raw? No one listened. And look at all these people. So unhappy, but not doing shit.

In the crowd, there was Amy—white halter top, tight jeans. She waved. "Brett!" she said, "It's all OK, dude."

What kind of wonderland was she living in? I wanted to push her to a locker, pin her on the metal door, squeeze her soft neck until the blood burst from her eyes. Hands quivering, I struggled with my locker combination. I punched my locker, and Mr. Wainscott, standing nearby, began the Approach—something our teachers did when they wanted to encourage us to articulate our feelings.

"It's OK," I said. "I'm OK, Mr. Wainscott." My voice cracked, thin and reedy.

A few days later, in the gym parking lot, I faced a banner that read "18 Days Until Homecoming." It was both foreboding and celebratory, the cheap plastic 18 barely hanging on, flapping. Zoe was in the office, and I was supposed to wait.

Of course, I had told her this would happen. During English IV, Ms. Sanders put Zoe in a group to "explore motifs" in *The Catcher in the Rye* using Facebook posts. Amy was in her group. Zoe bullied her, calling her "fucktard," her favorite, totally offensive word. Twice I told her to stop using it.

Amy texted Zoe—*Ugly slut*. It escalated.

In front of Amy, Zoe set up a Facebook page that read—SOMEONE BASH IN AMY BLAKE'S HEAD. She posted about Amy's "fat ass" and her secret desire to fuck her twin during conjugal visits. Everyone around them laughed, probably because it was a distraction from their otherwise depressing day.

Now Zoe was in the office, burning my phone up with texts I didn't answer. When she came out, she unloaded. The principal was concerned about her "social media attitude." Zoe's Twitter feed was populated with—*Yay! Fucking Chipotle!* But also, *I can't wait to kill all the disloyal bitches!* "There's a disconnect," said the principal.

The guidance counselor and Zoe's choir teacher, Jill Blevins, took her to the "Wallper," Wallerton High School's concession booth for froyo. They said, "Girls argue all the time." They suggested Zoe process her anger in healthy ways, like personal training or team sports.

"No offense, Ms. Blevins, but my life isn't *Mean Girls*," Zoe had said.

They told her to be nice. "Your digital face should match your real-life face. You're better than this."

But they still gave Zoe in-school suspension. She would miss a midterm, knocking her to a C in Algebra II. Her face grew a deep red, a swollen grape. Her parents would pay for college, and she nursed hope for the decent schools, maybe Oberlin.

Parked behind the factory, she said, "I'm going to bash Amy's face in for real." She clutched her messenger bag.

I was too tired to argue. I needed to get my own life together. How much could I do for everyone else? Something inside me burned, like a lit scrap of paper curls into itself.

"You got to do whatever you feel comfortable with," I said.

"I want you to help me," she said.

"No fucking way." I stared at the flood lamp and watched it waver and become unfocused.

☾

Amy showed up at the farm after hours one night. Dad was waiting for me to finish cutting checks, so I ground my teeth as they both stood at the desk. She asked why Zoe "wouldn't just let it go." I wanted her to leave, but silently fed checks in the tray, my back to her.

Dad told me to hurry, "It's getting late, bud." I acted dickish, the way guys do when they're demanding space. Or at least, they seem to in movies. I gave short answers, and Amy left confused. "Whatever, dude," she said. But I got the feeling she needed anything, even a "fuck-off."

Of course, I didn't tell Zoe about it at dinner at Texas Roadhouse. She'd pumped herself up to a boil talking about *CSI*, how sinew and cartilage required physical and emotional strength to sever. She didn't have it in her, really. Yet her thoughts disgusted me, and her monologues were repetitive. They sent me into this fog, like I listened to an album on repeat and then got up and didn't know where I was.

"I'm going to gut her like a deer," she said.

I dropped my fork. She didn't know what she was saying. She grew larger and larger, filling the room with her frustration and negative energy.

I changed the subject, pulled the homecoming card. Isn't that what all those teen flicks advise? A party would distract her, make frustration evaporate, replace it with glitter-covered euphoria.

"Sure," she said.

She went on about a documentary on a high school revenge where two girls planned to murder someone and created a fake timeline to throw off police. They got gas receipts from the drive to an alibi's house, wristbands from a concert taking place during the murder, photos of them in the crowd, posted to Facebook and scrubbed of metadata so the time was unclear.

"That's so crazy," I said.

She finally changed the subject. But I kept thinking about what she said.

A week later she'd gone to Ace. She opened her BMW's trunk to a box cutter, a Gator knife, two claw hammers, and a shovel, a roll of plastic, like the kind house-painters used, an industrial-sized container of bleach, and a cellophane-wrapped bundle of utility towels. She'd paid in cash, burned the receipt. She'd seen the boys' basketball coach, Mr. Pulaski, but he'd "been more interested in looking at my tits." I stood there staring into the trunk feeling chilled.

"Do not back out on me," she said.

"I've never been in this." I considered calling the cops.

"You love me. That means you're with me."

She pushed me to invite Amy to homecoming. All my attention was diverted to dealing with Dad, who was acting out emotionally. At the time, Dad told me not to visit his new apartment. *A working relationship is all we have, bud.* I just sat there, phone in hand, his last text unanswered.

"If I invite her," I said, "will you shut up about this?" I knew she wouldn't, but I wanted to be clear where I stood. I was thinking about my dad.

"Yeah. Duh," said Zoe.

Zoe pretended to befriend Amy again. She said if there was court testimony, she'd be off the hook. People at school would clamor to get on TV. "God no. They were all friends," they'd say.

I invited Amy to homecoming with Zoe, and she said, "Cool." I did not get it.

They both got ready at the Blake's trailer. I waited in the living room staring at the antler-mount gun rack, a squawking tube TV, and ugly floral furniture. Mrs. Blake sat on the sofa, her lips pursed, hands curled around the Bible in her lap.

Above the sofa hung framed Sears photos of both Amy and Kurt. Kurt wore his Eagle Scout uniform. His body looked Photoshopped on a version of Amy's head. So genetically similar. Balloons and a banner that read "Happy Birthday, Kurt" still stretched over the kitchen doorway, forgotten. Amy had said they celebrated his birthday via JPay Video Visit. Thirty people crowded into the living room to yell into the computer's tiny camera during Kurt's ten minutes of internet time. "Juvie is so weird," Amy told us.

Zoe mocked her comment for two days.

Waiting for the girls, I attempted conversation with Mrs. Blake. "How are you doing?"

"I thought you two broke up," said Mrs. Blake.

"We're all good friends now." I smiled.

"Doesn't make sense, taking two girls to homecoming."

"Well. Things are different these days. Everyone's friends now." But I was confused, too, and my voice sounded thin.

Both girls emerged from a nearby bedroom in homecoming dresses, their hair done in matching chignons. Amy still wore glasses, the manic pixie dream girl. Zoe's bandeau dress resembled the preliminary outfit of an '80s swimsuit model on photoshoot. It was a dick move assigning them fantasy roles, and fighting the images started a cluster headache. Yet I felt nailed to the floral chair, my eyes bugging like Kevin Spacey's in *American Beauty*.

Both girls twirled, groping each other for loose strings and errant straps. I pictured them together later, all hands, limbs, and swollen lips. I imagined being in the middle, obeying their demands. I made fists, squeezing my ragged nails into my palms. Yet I was responsible for the image. I entertained it.

When they stopped twirling, they stood silently as the TV swelled with applause.

"Wait a second," said Amy. She got a train-track of worry above her glasses. She walked over and turned off *American Idol*. My palms were slick with sweat.

"Mommy, take a video of me for Kurt."

"Mommy?" whispered Zoe. But Amy and Mrs. Blake hadn't heard. They were wrapped up in arranging the room, presumably with Kurt's favorite items: his rifle, a ceramic dog, a stack of his DVDs.

"Put his photo in the shot," said Mrs. Blake as she grabbed her iPad from the coffee table. She fussed with it and raised to record. "Go on."

Amy began stiffly lifting her arms as she danced, then spun. She stopped, put a foot on the coffee table. She looked confused. She giggled.

"Oh, he'll like that," said Mrs. Blake. "Twirl around a little more."

"Amy, we should probably get going," I said. End it, I thought. End it now. She seemed unaware we were still there.

"Oh," she said. Like they caught her coming out of

the shower. She went for her coat. "Be home in a while."
She walked out the door first, head down.

In the Pathfinder, Zoe told Amy some story about a
private after-homecoming party at Tony's grandparents'
lake house. "Baller" was the word she actually used. Zoe
had gone over to Tony's without me. I wasn't for sure
what Tony said, but I had picked up Zoe's phone the
night before and seen the text—*Can't wait to go all*
Dexter. Eye roll.

"Why at Tony's? He doesn't go here," said Amy.

"It's a secret party," said Zoe.

"At Tony's lake house? Have you been there? It's scary
as shit," said Amy.

"He's got it set up nice."

"Right." Amy smirked, unzipped her jacket and went
into the gym. She didn't believe a thing. I thought that
would be the end of it.

During homecoming, we took pulls off a stolen
bottle of Beefeater in the bathroom with dudes from
the basketball team. On the dance floor, everyone
seemed to pull a one-hitter from a tux jacket or a
tiny sequined purse.

By the time we loaded in the truck, I was near-drunk
and nauseated. The yellow lines on the highway and
the faint outline of wooded expanse of Hocking Hills
felt dreamy, like those A.A. Milne books Dad read
when I was a kid, all footprints and paths lost over
muted green. The girls had climbed in the back to get
drinks, pausing for selfies, laughing, arms wrapped
around each other. They snapped pics, tipping a new
bottle of JD, and I thought how much better it was
just to get drunk.

"Let's go to the pond," said Zoe. Her mouth was pursed, a hard line in the rearview mirror, her expression meaningful. I tried to focus on the highway to avoid locking eyes.

Amy suddenly straightened. She'd been reaching into my cooler for something other than hard liquor, a PBR. Up to that point she'd been giddy, explosive with joy. But now she assumed the pragmatic smirk she used in describing her tattoo or defending her brother. "You guys can go, maybe swing by my mom's and drop me. It's all cool."

"No," said Zoe. She punched Amy's shoulder. "It's like ten o'clock. Early. Don't be such a pussy."

Amy said, "No. I mean, I'm not into it. Maybe take me home."

Zoe turned it up real fast. "Don't be like that. You've been a bitch all year. Let's bury the hatchet, have something good to remember." Zoe pulled her knees to her chest and picked polish from a fingernail.

Why had I thought I could make everybody have fun? Wasn't I owed something without strings, something outside clipping beaks in a cloud of iodine disinfectant? We could get drunk, at least. In the rearview, I could see Amy was halfway hazy, her thigh bare, bird tattoo flying up her calf. It was so purposely stylized and beautiful on her. I told myself to stop staring, gripped the steering wheel.

The pond was a couple miles up the highway. If I asked, she'd go. "I feel like swimming," I said.

"All right," said Amy. "If everyone's going to be cool about it."

Zoe lay her head on Amy's shoulder.

Maybe it would be all right. They could "bury the hatchet."

I turned off the highway, the truck pitching over the rutted dirt road. A new sign at the pond read "The Ozer's. Be respectful." One of the Ozers had left a trash can to encourage tresspassers to recycle. Moonlight glinted from the painted surface of a swim raft bobbing in the middle of the pond, wind ruffled the dark water.

Determined to smooth things, I acted irritated, told them to "do some swimming, already." I thought my anger might create space, distract them. The girls ignored me, pulled off their dresses. Amy laid her glasses on a picnic table. "Watch those," she said. The frames looked bent and beaten.

They splashed into the pond.

I was unbuttoning my shirt, but they told me to stay so they could talk. I sat on the dock, watched as they swam toward the middle with strong strokes, as if chasing each other. I lay back, looked at the stars.

I thought about growing up in Wayne National Forest, how the woods, river, and lakes held specific memories. The undulating hills carried my childhood of hiking and camping in open fields, harriers swooping overhead. Nearby I'd hunted with Dad, a mile from the dairy farm and the Andersons' land. Zoe may not have done all that, but Amy definitely did.

I thought of the unmanageable sledge of wastewater. Dad spent hours drinking beer at the storage barn with his employees, but he never wanted to hike the river basin or fish or hunt anymore. At night he parked the work truck at the lagoon, which had lately filled with algae blooms. I didn't know what he did there. Maybe an unscheduled inspection would unhinge Dad, force him to remember something better. Someone just had to call. I already felt the phone's weight. Shitty as it was, it could be anonymous.

The splashing had stopped, and I heard only crickets. I sat up. At the far end of the pond, yards from the raft, there was only one head above water. The head disappeared, re-emerged, disappeared again.

I jumped in still wearing half my tux. The freezing water stung. My lungs expanded, arms pumping, as I swam quick strokes. I met Amy bobbing above the surface, her chin skimming the water, clearly working to keep from sinking. She labored for breath. She said, "Zoe came at me. She was trying to hold my head under. I just pushed her down once." She uttered it without inflection.

I dove down. Past a few feet, it was all silt and black water. Toward the bottom, I skimmed soft weeds. I came up, dove again, swimming fast, spreading my arms. I collided with Zoe, my lungs burning, and ferried her towards the moonlight. It had only been seconds but felt longer. I kicked and pulled, her hair spreading over the surface, her limbs like plastic. She'd grown cold, but it might have been the chilled air.

On the way to the hospital, Amy held Zoe's head in the crook of her arm as if nursing a baby. Zoe hadn't said a word, hadn't opened her eyes since I attempted mouth-to-mouth. I couldn't tell how serious she was about being sick. Her chest did sound rattly. I'd heard people could dry drown hours after rescue.

Amy had that lost look of a kid on a long-distance

road trip. She stared out the window. In the moonlight, the forest branches were black against the sky. I wanted to make sure she was with me. It felt safer if she wouldn't tell. "Do you like the national forest or those private lands better?"

She paused, and I thought she was going to share an intimate memory—a camping trip, a hunting trip. I needed to hear something like that.

"I'm not sure I have an opinion. I feel like a ghost," she said.

She surprised me, but I said, "Me, too."

TELL ME

Greg is telling that story again at the office party, the one where our spokesdog, Biscuit, awakens her owner with a tug to the sleeve before the ceiling collapses in flames. The sales associates have stopped flirting and have abandoned a ransacked snack table. They sip wine from Solo cups and fold their arms across company golf shirts. They appear a little awed, even as their dogs roam the crowd sniffing paper plates, hands, and occasionally thighs.

"We would have gone bankrupt without that dog," says Greg. His sport jacket and tight jeans shave off ten years, but lately he looks like he came off a bender. His skin is gray and slack.

"It's true." His business partner, Joe, has worn that same red fleece all week, and his tape measure has worn a hole in the back pocket.

"My mom thinks I work for that pet franchise with the dog from *The Today Show*," says a team lead. "Are you saying Biscuit didn't do any of that?"

Andrew, the regional manager, is engrossed in his phone. My phone buzzes with his text. It reads simply, *The Today Show*.

"Plenty of dogs save their owners," says Greg. "They run through fires, pull children from lakes."

"Now, don't bullshit them." Joe laughs. "That dog didn't save anyone." He points to the banner overhead. It has an image of Biscuit, a lab with huge wet eyes. "She was afraid of thunder."

"Hey. Who knows what that dog has gone on to do," says Greg.

Several sales associates exchange looks. Some laugh. But it's that umph laugh, like heartburn or acknowledging a pun.

"And in two weeks we'll open our third store." Greg starts clapping. Everyone joins him, and the dogs get whipped up and cut the tension with explosive barks.

Was it convivial? Yes. Did it feel like we were a big work family? It did.

Greg catches my eye as I refill my chardonnay. Maybe he's actually sick and not hungover. I am about to walk over and offer ibuprofen and Emergen-C from my purse, but he points at my face, his thumb and forefinger forming a gun and pulls the trigger. He smirks. So I force a smile.

If you suspect your boss is a criminal, like most people, you would call your mom. My mom died when I was young. Pancreatic cancer. This is far lonelier than I let on to friends. You need family, one person who has your back because they've known you since childhood.

Without my mom, that someone is my brother, Elliot. But we only talk once a year. He is a cop who loves jawing about his job, so he squeezes all his stories into one call. He never seems to want to hang up. During our last conversation, he detailed a swatting—twelve officers surrounding a guy's house, creeping along the hydrangea, aiming at this guy's open windows. Officers took cover behind squad cars. Elliot described the sobering feel of leveling a .45 on a man. He corrects himself: "A drug dealer. This was a vendetta swatting."

My brother possesses an unswerving confidence in his own judgment. He is never conflicted. Even his obligatory holiday texts are humble brags.

Ate too much turkey. Time to do a 5K run.

Polished off a bottle of wine last night with a retired senator. Doing a cleanse today.

The whole family hiked ten miles to flat rock. Sprained my ankle. Totally worth it.

Elliot wants to jail all the drug dealers, and then the Wall Street crooks. He is a CPA. He plans to work in the financial crimes division and "catch a Bernie Madoff." I nearly roll my eyes out of my head whenever he says this, but obviously he is the person to call.

Elliot greets me with, "Hey. How ya doing? I'm just starting my weight-lifting routine here."

I cut right to it. "I'm pretty sure my boss is embezzling." I explain how Greg has me write huge checks without a single corresponding invoice. Essentially, he just takes out money whenever he feels like it. He *claims* he's buying products COD. When I emailed both Greg and Joe saying every expense needs an invoice, Greg replied-all with, "Do you even know what you're doing?"

"What a dirtball," Elliot says. He's breathless like he's already started some serious curls. "You have to have invoices. I bet he's overextended."

"He just bought a new sports car. Like a GT or something," I say.

"That does not sound good." He whispers his rep counts.

"Damn it. What should I do?" I had wanted Elliot to say embezzlement was rare and required deep criminal knowledge. Greg seems generally sleazy, not a mastermind. Instead, Elliot says, "Quit." But then he pauses his rep count. "You don't sign the checks, right?"

"I do sign the checks! I do everything—bookkeeping, HR, web design, anything they can't afford to hire for. It's a startup."

Elliot lets out a huge breath like he has moved on to bench presses. "Sounds like his partner is clueless, too," he says. I hear the high ring of metal hitting metal as he releases a weight.

Here's where I pull back. "Joe's a good guy," I say. "He was vocal about me getting a good salary." There's a line here.

"You can't spend it in jail," he says.

"Are you quoting a movie?"

Elliot spouts dialogue from old crime movies whenever he doesn't know what to say. He started it like ten years ago, after he had his first daughter and grew anxious under the weight of parenting. It seems a little OCD. But he's pretty good. Some of the actors he mimics are obvious, like—Humphrey Bogart or Peter Lorre. Others are obscure—your Ralph Meeker, your Clifton Webb.

"I should go," I say.

☾

At the store, Andrew nicks his finger with the box-cutter opening a case of dog treats and acts like it's the end of the world. "Goddamn, why package this like a nuclear bomb?"

On Fridays, we match his product to my invoices and have lunch at a basement pizza place next door. He curses so often and so creatively, I'm only mildly surprised he yells "motherfucker" and sucks his finger before I even get my coat off.

Andrew has angular features and is sometimes goofy, which I like. But our work flirtation is likely fueled by boredom. He complains about his girlfriend, but he's obviously into whatever they have going.

"You're early?" He wipes his forehead with his sleeve.

"Joe asked me to bring over bonuses," I say.

"So we should hop a plane to Mexico?" He hands me a box-cutter.

"Or drive to Canada." I carefully cut the plastic on a pallet of Wilderness kibble.

"I'm sure Canada has a stronger extradition policy." He stands, straightens his T-shirt. "I'm just fucking kidding. Why are you looking at me like that?"

I come clean, even though it's stressful to tell him we both might be out of a job soon. I ease into it.

"Greg made me write another check yesterday. Fifteen thousand. No invoice. He's taken out a hundred grand in a month."

Andrew leans against the shelves and lets his shoulders sink. With the buildout of this new store, we both thought Greg might straighten up. "Damnit!" says Andrew.

It's really disappointing. We were in on the ground level of a massive pet store chain. Holistic pet supplies were sure to take off in Atlanta, Denver, Seattle, San Francisco. We would have this work family and a recognizable brand in every town, so your Pekingese could enjoy a life free from skin conditions and matted fur. Your Puli and Dandie Dinmont Terrier could have an all-natural diet as it would in the wild. We were going to make the world more goddamn delightful, one light-up toy at a time.

"He's a fucking douche, man. He probably came out of the womb a douche, and his mom was like, 'Dammit, why did I give birth to such a douche?'" Andrew bends down and yanks boxes from the case. He throws them onto the shelf. "I would never run a business like this."

"Joe's probably liquidating part of his retirement to cover this place, even as we speak." I return to unwinding the plastic from the pallet. When Andrew doesn't answer my trash talk with more trash talk, I look up to see his face frozen in a scowl.

I stand up. "What?"

There's a light touch on my arm, and I hear a voice. "Did you bring the bonuses?"

"Hey Joe," I say. "Didn't see you there."

"I'd like to pass them out here first." His smile is faint, and I can't tell if he heard me. He's making eye contact, but his brow is cinched with worry. I'm an asshole.

TELL HIM, Andrew mouths the words.

I lift my purse and pull out the envelope of checks. I hand it over. "Everybody appreciates this," I say. "Your sacrifice."

Andrew rolls his eyes, but I keep my mouth shut.

☾

My brother struggles with sleep and admits that in the wee hours he binges on *Cops, CSI,* and, of course, old detective movies. When the fatigue accumulates, he takes a hardcore sleep aid, and, around two or so, sleepwalks to the kitchen and eats a leftover casserole or pizza or a whole Tupperware of cookies, until my sister-in-law finds him and ushers him back to their room. So it isn't surprising at midnight when I get the text—*What are you doing about your crooked boss?*

Elliot knows how to project a big-brother/cop type tone when it suits him. I always went to him for advice in high school—passing classes, getting some guy's attention. But we aren't that kind of family anymore. I don't need an open chain of texts to make me feel obligated.

To be honest, the irony of him becoming a cop this last year sticks in my craw. He acts as though prosecuting criminals has always been his calling. But the first time all our family secrets came out, he took my dad's side.

On the way to church, I shared details it took me months to confess. Elliot looks perfectly glassy-eyed, like he will be sick over the steering wheel. He slowly sinks the gas pedal, pushing us to ninety. He ignores the occasional hum of the rumble strip as the tires stray.

I want my brother to concede what he's seen. But I come out aggressive. "I hope you don't mind the whole church knowing," I tell him.

"What are you talking about?" he says.

"I'm going to report him."

"That's a felony." He looks horrified. "It means serious prison time."

When I don't answer, Elliot knows I'm serious. He yanks the steering wheel toward the service road and floors it through a speed zone. He cuts, tires screeching, into a Ruby Tuesday. His speed launches him over a curb, and he drives through some bushes before hitting a parking barrier. He has a death-grip on the steering wheel. He begins to cough. He opens the door. He throws up on the asphalt.

Two men in jeans and flannels hurry over to check out the situation. From their raised eyebrows, they clearly believe Elliot is drunk. It is on the tip of my tongue to spill our story, to tell them the whole situation. Instead, I stare straight ahead. My brother says he's fine and they take him at his word. One guy hands him a wad of napkins from his to-go bag before walking on. "Take it easy," he says over his shoulder.

Elliot wipes his face.

"If you tell the police, you're no longer my sister," he says.

So perhaps Joe and I will report Greg to the police together. That sounds likely.

I blow smoke through the barred window of our office, a unit in a refurbished cold-storage building stuffed with boxes of pet food samples and three oversized metal desks. Mine is at the front, and this morning I probably sat for ten minutes rehearsing my opening—*Hey, Joe, I think your partner is stealing. Hey, Joe, your high school buddy is a thief. Hey, Joe, your friend of twenty years is actively ruining your life.* I hear footfalls in the stairwell and chuck the cigarette through the bars. I have to run to unlock the door.

"Sorry I'm late," says Joe. He shakes the rain from his baseball cap over the rubber mat. Usually he brings a box of cinnamon rolls and a caddy of coffee to our monthly meetings, but today he's empty-handed, and his eyes are red.

I slide into my seat, holding the reports. "You OK?" I ask.

He sinks into the office chair and rubs his forehead. He takes the reports like he needs something to hold, like he doesn't know what to do with his hands. "I'm going to be honest," he says. "We can't make payroll."

"There's money in the account," I say. This is the time to tell him.

"I wrote a check for the buildout before looking at the account," he says. It's clear he's bewildered. He shakes his head. "I guess we just needed way more product than I anticipated."

He really has no idea. How is that possible? I can barely resist the urge to shout—GREG WITHDREW YOUR MONEY. HE MADE CHECKS OUT TO HIMSELF. HE DOESN'T CARE ABOUT YOU.

"Don't worry. I'm going to meet with Greg and see about getting a line of credit; otherwise, I'm going to liquidate some of my own funds," he says.

"Don't."

He smiles a little. "Payroll can't be late. But I might have to let some floor staff go."

This feels like a punch to the gut. "Joe, listen."

☾

Repeating violence—a fire, a fight, a rape—holds a moment of release. But if the story isn't offered, it can feel like a thick worm pulled from your throat, like the segmented body writhing over your tongue. For a long time, I hadn't talked about it.

When Elliot asks the women's Bible study leader to invite me to a prayer breakfast, I am livid. "I have a therapist," I say. She's an empathetic listener, free through the school, unconnected to our family.

I decide not to tell this tight-lipped deaconess anything. But there she is when I arrive at church with Elliot and Dad. She touches my forearm. She knows something, but I feel certain Elliot has left Dad out of it. Some shadowy figure, a troubled neighbor kid, an older teen babysitter, has become the shiftless person to pin it on.

The deaconess's whisper is minty. "Jesus's love has no limits." She offers to buy me coffee and "study the word sometime" before I head to college.

She leads me to a seat, with her amazingly tight grip. Her Bible study group fills the first row. I squeeze in beside another teen, a girl who reeks of cigarettes, and who will eventually trace the cross hatched scars on my forearm during the opening prayer.

And the altar call. The altar call. People raise their hands in surrender to a sermon on forgiveness or repentance or peace or something. The pastor clutches a microphone, eyes closed, and testifies with palm upraised. "Surely, God's grace is here," he says. And the bass comes in with the first few notes of *At the*

Cross sucking the air from the room and makeing the hairs on my arms and legs stand up.

This Sunday, it seems all for Elliot. He slowly walks to the altar. And he cries, and people cry with him, and other men, some our age, grasp his shoulder and hang on. Elliot lifts his folded prayer-hands to his face for two hymns, though altar calls usually last only one.

What could he want God to do about this?

Elliot stands, and turns so I finally see his whole face and it is blank, like a huge burden is gone, like he can float out of the building and right down the street, and into the rest of his life. He's given it to Christ, of course, and everyone around him cries with joy. He doesn't even have to say who needs atonement in our family.

I stare at the altar and think, well, that's convenient.

One morning before work, I open an email from the accountant asking for the quarterlies. The answer to stopping Greg's embezzlement becomes obvious.

I get up and go to CVS for a thumb drive. I feel like a sleepwalker going through rote actions, my intuition as a guide. I will cut out early so Greg won't have the chance to fire me. I can't bear that. At the office, I photocopy bank statements, cancelled checks, stock certificates and reconciliations on the ancient copier, and shove a set in my purse. I call a courier to pick up the other set. Then, I email a full explanation of Greg's theft to the accountant, who is legally required to do something. For good measure, I copy the head of the firm, whose name I have to pull from their website.

Someone will call Greg or Joe and broach the subject

of embezzlement. I watch YouTube videos of cats and wait. I don't know why. Maybe I hope Joe will hear first and call. Of course, I couldn't tell him the whole story, not to his face. At 2 p.m., I pack my stuff, put on my coat, and turn off the lights.

As I shoulder my purse, I hear the teeth of keys in the lock. Light from the soda machine spills in from the hallway.

"Where are you going?" says Greg. He looks mildly surprised.

"I'm heading out," I say.

He blocks the door, his body outlined in blue from the soda machine. I grip two keys between my fingers. Why am I afraid? He's never been physically aggressive. I just imagine if he is willing to screw over his friend, he might be a sociopath.

"It's not even three o'clock. But OK. You're knocking off early," says Greg.

"Andrew needs me to stock at the South Loop store." I hope this will move him, but he just stands there.

"Listen, Carrie. You've been in over your head for a while. We're letting you go," he says. There's that smirk from the staff party.

I'm shaking, but I still say, "Fuck you." I hope this will get him to move, but he doesn't. His face is smooth and shiny with sweat. His mouth is open. He smells like the whiskeys he likely downed at a business lunch.

"Better hope nothing's missing in this office," he says.

"Can you move?" My pitch is so high it surprises me.

He jumps out of the way as if he hasn't even thought about the dynamic until now. He has the nerve to look offended.

Outside, the cool air hits me, and I pause on the sidewalk. In Greg's reserved parking spot is his GT, all chrome and bright yellow. Keys between my fingers, I consider running them the length of the car, the yellow paint curling like a ribbon. But I just stand there.

Above me, the office is lit a murky white against the overcast autumn afternoon. He has probably come to throw away check copies or change the books. But I already have confirmation the courier made the delivery. I imagine Greg ripping open drawers and binders, trying to locate the statements.

Eventually, it grows depressing to stand there and watch a window, and I head home.

Even before that uncomfortable day at church, I'd decided to do it.

I had an airtight plan—pack a bag, say I'm sleeping at a friend's, park a few blocks away, walk up the street wearing my dark navy jacket.

Dad will be watching baseball in the downstairs family room. He will have dozed by the sixth inning.

I could have burned down our house, so his skin crackled and leapt and whistled as it caught. My brother wasn't home. Who would suspect me? But TV taught me there is always a trail of microbes and receipts and neighbors without blinds who stand in front of their windows at night.

Our house is built into the Allegheny foothills, an ugly split-level with two bedroom windows like eye-holes in a mask. I pull the spray paint from my bag, even before I get up the drive. I think of the adolescent girls in our neighborhood, a couple are just now ten. Dad rarely goes outside, but he could ask them to cut his lawn or walk our dog or some other bullshit. He could give one of them a gift. He gave me a bike.

The door of our two-car garage is bright white in the flood lamp.

I stretch on the balls of my feet and follow the paint line to crouch on the cement, keeping the letters even and tall, so everyone will see it after passing through the subdivision entrance. I stand back to survey the squashed letters with slight unease—RAPIST.

I knock on the door at the rear entrance of the new store knowing Andrew will be counting receipts. Even through the tinted safety glass, his face appears bloodless, and he holds up a finger before releasing the locks. He has one hand shoved in his hoodie pocket. I see the box cutter bulging from the other pocket, which seems over the top. "I was afraid you were Greg. They haven't changed the lock on this back door," he says.

I hand him a bag. "Joe wanted me to bring over this new security camera so the guy can install it tomorrow. Are you done? Want a drink?"

"Sure," he says. He returns to a stack of receipts, pivoting so stiffly, I wonder what news he has to tell me. "Do you mind if I smoke?" he says.

"Of course, not."

He lights a cigarette, and I slide onto the edge of the desk. He gathers the bank bag and the rubber bands he's using to bind rolls of quarters. He says, "Man, when Joe changed that first lock, I thought it was over."

"Yeah. He was in the office on the phone with his lawyers."

Cigarette clinging to his lips, Andrew makes a hammock of his sweatshirt and loads in rolls of change. "Then Greg comes around 8 a.m. Wants to talk to me."

I shove my hands in my pockets. "It's not like you're going to unlock the doors for him."

"No way," says Andrew. He kneels beside the safe.

I imagine Greg standing at the glass doors in the middle of the South Loop, face inches from the glass, his shoulders tense as he starts yelling to open the door. Unsurprising.

Andrew stuffs the rolls of change into the tiny safe. "He said you were lying. You didn't know what you were doing. You lost the paperwork. All that bullshit. Right through the motherfucking door."

"Wow," I say.

Andrew returns to the desk to stuff the cash into a bank bag, a few stacks of tens and twenties. He pulls a single twenty from a stack. "Petty cash. For drinks," he says. He actually shakes the bill at me. I suddenly feel nauseated.

Andrew returns to the safe and shoves the bag inside. "Like I'd buy that crap about you. You're straight as an arrow." He crushes his cigarette on the table. "Seriously. Thanks for saving our asses, though."

"No problem," I say.

He slides into his coat and pulls the keys from his pocket. "I'm so glad we don't have to listen to that douche's same five stories anymore. He was the worst."

"Yeah. The worst."

☾

In some ways, Elliot has always been tough. At least, he's always been comfortable in his own body. And he's always been fast.

The foothills of the Alleghenies are slick and nearly impossible to run in the winter. But Elliot leans so far forward in his sprint, he appears perpendicular to the asphalt, as if with a little effort he can fly over the street, grazing it lightly with his fingertips.

Though my lungs burn with frozen air, I haven't fallen behind, not even a yard. On our last leg home he'll shout "You got this" as we race to the garage. But he always reaches it first, smacking the wood hard enough to rattle the chains of the automatic door.

He has been bugging me to revive our morning runs for weeks. When he saw me sneak from the bathroom, crossing my arms over my chest to hide the red hatches, he said, "Tomorrow morning."

Anyway, the sound of Dad's early activities—the whistling and the tinkling of silverware against a cereal bowl—have awakened in me a desire to shiv him at the breakfast table. The tension has only risen as each morning Dad absently taps his coffee mug with his spoon, long after the milk has dissolved. I agree to a run.

Elliot and I run the side streets which go the whole winter unplowed. Our route drops onto a service road which we pound to the highway. We always get coffee and a sandwich with egg and country ham at a place for truckers. We will eat outside and sit on the picnic tables beneath the truck stop sign.

At this moment, we can still say anything. And this is the point where I hope he'll share my grief. Witness it. In a few months, I'll have a therapist and it will all come out. Right now, all I have to say is——I want out of my own skin.

I need to—
    put my hand in a car door
    slam a hot iron to my face
    jump off an overpass
    peel the skin down to the white fat with a fillet knife
    soak in bleach
    stick my fingers in a food processor
    drink a mug of antifreeze

I need, for just a few minutes, to not be in this body. This body, it seems, is the source of my trouble.

Our steps wind down as we reach the picnic tables at the far end of the parking lot, where we pant for breath. "I need to see a counselor," I say.

Elliot has been going on and on about his girlfriend, who will eventually become my sister-in-law.

"Elliot," I say. "Dad molested me." I slowly explain the when and the how, but I'm waiting for affirmation. Did I think of yelling for him? Yes. But I was nine, ten, and eleven, and Dad whispered so many threats. His large body became a mass of hair and sweat and endless flesh. I clawed at the sheets. Yes. But I never seemed able to fill my lungs enough to scream.

"You didn't hear a thing?" I say. "You didn't hear a door creak? Nothing?"

"No," he says. "No." He slowly shakes his head. It looks like he won't stop this ridiculous action.

I sit on the wet picnic table. Elliot's face drains. He

tries to sit beside me but misses the slick edge and falls. He stands, but slips on the gravel again and catches himself with one hand, looking like a sad acrobat. "So bad." he says. "So bad."

A woman getting donuts with her boyfriend walks over and asks if I'm OK. She clearly imagines my brother is an abusive boyfriend. I tell her it's fine. Though she's uncertain, she walks to her car.

Elliot gives up on sitting and paces for minutes, tennis shoes crunching the gravel, his arms anchored to the back of his head like he's stretching. He will talk to our dad. Yes. He will talk to Dad.

I can see by his expression, his resolve is already slipping, though, even as he says what he'll do. So I hold him to put him at ease.

LETTER TO AMANDAS

My friend Brandon has packed his friend's Jeep
with provisions of Sno Balls, dried turkey, Finlandia.
Observing the heaped vehicle, and considering the
2,700 miles to California, I am reminded of the idea
that we are like goldfish adapting to our space. My
friend beckons with a freestyle stroke as if he is about
to marathon-swim the English Channel. In his other
hand, he grips a Holga he would rather wear around
his neck, in the spirit of "adventuring."

People call him handsome and Scandinavian-looking.
It bothers me that there might be an implied relationship between these two ideas. But he has wide
cheekbones and blond curls. He's one friend I can sit
with and "share a silence," a relationship quality people
seem to admire. He likes small dogs, especially my pug.
Other than this, I like him for reasons I can't articulate.

I tell him about Tarrare, who was tormented by his
appetite and pillaged gutter heaps for inedible objects.
Tarrare was employed by General De Beauharnais as a
courier-spy during France's revolutionary wars. Because
of his wide gullet, he was able to swallow a wooden
box filled with secret information. This did not help
him when the enemy captured him and forced him to
wait until his bowels moved. Brandon leans closer for

157

the disgusting part. "Then what happened?" he says. He enjoys his clichéd remark. Bits of potato chips fly from his mouth. I continue, but he interrupts me for a pit stop and Red Bulls. He drinks one, talks fast, and is impossible to understand above the wind-roar and gear shifting. But I focus on the syntax pattern—Noun. Verb. Noun. Noun. Verb. Although, I know it is impertinent and rude to recast his ideas this way.

Brandon works at a Fotomat in the same building as a laundromat. The place is called Matt's Mats, and Matt has barely given him a vacation. In fact, he clocked him—in the jaw. But they're cousins so they made amends. Brandon incessantly recommends *The Act of Seeing With One's Own Eyes* because he saw it last week. Then he adds a description of himself leaned over the toilet, burrito revisiting his throat, his passing thoughts of re-scrubbing the toilet. This wears on me. I think about writing an email to an ex-coworker I barely like and have forgotten to answer. She needs help finding a job, and I'm sort of obligated because she appears desperate and has taken the time to write me. I hate that I feel this way.

I have taken this trip to dispose of my marriage trinkets, affectionately known as Minkets. Brandon says no, but this will happen in a helluva drunken fire on the desert, preferably at a roadside motel, causing the people inside to say, "Oh, what's that?" Brandon's response is obtuse because he adores fires. He wants persuasion.

Victrolas are tinny, and stereopticons produce only passable 3-D images. In Victorian England, stereopticons were one of the only forms of entertainment—self-aggrandizing pictures of women playing cards in their living rooms. Pictures I would refer to as obsessive.

Brandon tells me to stop thinking about "intellectual things." He has exploded with annoyance, a behavior I describe to him as pleasantly sexy. I don't tell him I have emailed Will who lives in California. I have not heard from Will in three years, because we are "that kind of friends." I guess, the silent kind, and the kind who have engaged in countertop sex—so, not very intimate either. "Hey Will, I am coming to visit. Stop. Please have my favorite chips. Stop. I now know many interesting people, so I have more to talk about. Stop." Though it is not a telegraphed message, I insert the words stop because Will appreciates the obvious. Sex is my other goal for this trip.

Even though we stayed in a hotel and watched *The Third Man*, computers warming our thighs for three hours, I haven't emailed the friend who requested help finding a job. I also realize I am halfway through a piece and roughly two days in fictional-letter-time has passed. I hate that it engages me in a self-involved mental row. When I mention my forgotten letters, Brandon says his ex-girlfriend, whom he still wants to get back with, only trusts written apologies. Even with this key information, he is unable to rouse himself to action.

"I can't believe you brought it," he says. The "it" we refer to sits like a Yeti in the backseat. "It" is a garment bag filled with relics my ex saved—old movie tickets, Halloween masks of the Dead Kennedys, the sleeves for his favorite DVDs. The combined bulk of the letters written on the backs of college posters, advertising his favorite bands like My Life with the Thrill Kill Kult, makes it un-zippable.

America loves memoir. In fact, it is a part of our forefathers' favorite communication. I blame the early Americans' need to form Puritanical ways—one might call them 'habits of mind'—something I will never possess. I also blame the personal reverberations in Emerson, Thoreau and Whitman. Everyone loves solipsism. Do they see some larger eye following their constructed pilgrimage on Earth? Brandon leans out the window and barks at a girl biking on the berm. Colluding, I slow and roll down his window. She says nothing, her face red as we pass.

The first night we spend in the vehicle, we sleep in separate sleeping bags, but when it drops below 50 degrees, he pastes his body against me, spoons, and exhales barbecue hot-fry breath all night. When I ask him about our "lay-together," he says, "What?" At a public rest area, Brandon attempts to kiss a pine tree. Then he humps it. I run my fingers through my sweaty hair. Shampoo. The kind you haven't heard of, in an amber bottle. Hotel shampoo. We should stop. I have another minor thought that in a cave we would shape-shift to our favorite animals.

A familiar has all the properties of a messenger—and it accomplishes things the silent owner cannot. In English lore, a familiar can also shape-shift. Because one animal is not enough and I have mood swings, I long to be a cat-bat. Brandon is completely uninterested in this, but has offered to go down on me.

We end up in this cave on this hillside. You actually have to go down several miles of dirt road. The road appears to go absolutely nowhere, and if you had car trouble you would be fucked. The potholes pop us up to the Jeep's roof. A silo marks the way with a painted wooden sign that reads "Cave," and this sends us both into hysterics. In a field there is a trellis façade, a weed-infested barn and a parking lot. A sign reads "Misty Waters Cave," and it is very green and hilly and what some people would probably call "verdant." I walk past the barn and feel him behind me. As he runs ahead of me shouting, "Murder, murder," I am irritated and irascible.

The sign on the door reads "Closed." Yes, I understand the significance of the cave. But I view this cave as more of a pool—not the public kind where you could get a rash or see the different incarnations of human aging, but the kind where your one rich friend goes out of town, and he or she asks you to house-sit. The indoor, Daddy Warbucks kind. If you have a dog, he can jump in, too. So this really isn't a pool, either, but a gift without attachments. Brandon gets up, walks to the cave, and takes pictures with his Holga. He suggests we lie down right there and make an effort to undo my loneliness. This is both impossible and sweet. How could anything that lasted for five years be undone? But I don't mention it because it would only make him experience my depression. Instead, I take him up on his offer to go down on me.

Amanda, I am curious if you remember the time we talked of cohabitating platonically. Well, moving into a shared space without windows would be completely depressing. Moving into a space without walls would encourage accidents. I've lived in a space without locks.

This is fine if you know someone. I might even suggest it as a future outward demonstration of intimacy. But with a stranger, it could set you on edge. Then you get pink eye, and what are you going to do? You can drink milk with drops of bourbon to calm you. Call your mother. Watch the BBC version of *Pride and Prejudice* to comfort yourself with its codified behavior systems. But eventually, you wish you had locks.

Because he is energized by awkward tension, Brandon wishes he actually met my ex. He parks the car on the side of the road when we talk. After twenty minutes, he appears bored, pulls out an old derringer and fires at a groundhog. Yes, I was surprised too, given his affection for dogs that are roughly the same size. But sometimes your friend's behavior is like messages through a string and can, broke up and unintelligible, leaving you to wonder about the source. The sun is high, and he punctuates the explosions with whoops. He's not aiming.

If I wrote my ex a letter, he probably wouldn't answer. I know this because I wrote my ex a letter and he didn't answer. Brandon has scaled the side of a canyon without equipment. At the top, he raises his arms as if he has truly conquered something. I still hold the empty ketchup bottle and napkins from our picnic. Suddenly, I imagine I am three hundred pounds and balding, and this makes me want to shape-shift into something fanciful, a dragon, perhaps. I move the meaty parts of my arms as if I will, then worry someone will see me. Then I get angry at myself for having these thoughts. "Come up here," yells Brandon. "It's nice." He looks exactly as he did in the car, windblown, godlike and fiery.

As we look out the darkened window, Brandon holds my hand. Despite his sweaty palm, I feel comforted. He leans toward me as we stare at the flickering neon sign and create nocturnal stories about watery, ephemeral places, a Shangri La of sorts, only with naiads, of both sexes, and bartenders to serve us drinks. He softly touches my arm. We are interrupted by a metallic crash outside the door. For some reason, he doesn't get tired of hearing my stories.

We decide not to visit Will. Will will be OK with it. At a 7-11, Brandon runs in and out of the doors to hear the whir and to irritate me. When the 7-11 guy says something to him, Brandon doesn't respond. In Brandon's defense, it is hard to tell what this quiet guy says. "Stop. Don't do that. Figs."

I imagine if we drive too long in one day, the highway will inspire flight, like the concert poster I just released through the open window. A flying, tumbling paper. I imagine a horizon in the darkness, wires, a helmet, mountains and something unnamable, a couple of chairs and a hotel again. Brandon and I break bread, as they say, crackers and dry peanut butter. The wind picks up around the Jeep's door, as Brandon cradles my palm to deliver the food. He points out a sign, a lone message that has been spray-painted and makes little sense.

Instead of a cave, we find a band shelter in a park, unzip the sleeping bags and lie down. The blue paint is chipped to a rust color, the cement floor damp. Welcome pilgrim, thou hast come far. In this case, I have written many emails, which I will call letters, with all the time-commitment and connotation of intimacy.

Carefully considered intimacy. I would write: Brandon's skin is soft, his mouth dry. As our lips touch, I think of different words for letters: missives, Morse code, telegrams, sonnets. With him inside me, I say nothing. I lean back and contain many words.

Yours,
Dearest Amanda

MOON CITY PRESS
SHORT FICTION AWARD WINNERS

Cate McGowan, *True Places Never Are*
2014

Laura Hendrix Ezell, *A Record of Our Debts*
2015

Michelle Ross, *There's So Much They Haven't Told You*
2016

Kim Magowan, *Undoing*
2017

Amanda Marbais, *Claiming a Body*
2018

CPSIA information can be obtained
at www.ICGtesting.com
Printed in the USA
FSHW022056060619
58818FS